Masterpieces of Wit, Whimsy and Satire

A saint struggles with the greatest of all temptations: daily life.

A genius proposes a world inventory of genius to create a better life, but he cannot bear the company.

Family life trembles with enough animus to bring down an elephant.

A woman leaves her husband and enters the red velvet map of a new life.

Books by Donald Barthelme

Amateurs
City Life
The Dead Father
Great Days
Sadness
Unspeakable Practices, Unnatural Acts

Published by POCKET BOOKS

DONALD BARTHELME

Sadness

PUBLISHED BY POCKET BOOKS NEW YORK

Except for "The Sandman" and "Träumerei," all of the stories in this book appeared originally in *The New Yorker*, some in slightly different form.

"The Sandman" appeared originally in *The Atlantic*.

POCKET BOOKS, a Simon & Schuster division of
GULF & WESTERN CORPORATION
1230 Avenue of the Americas, New York, N.Y. 10020

Published by arrangement with Farrar, Straus & Giroux, Inc.
Library of Congress Catalog Card Number: 72-84774

ISBN: 0-671-83204-2

First Pocket Books printing October, 1980

10 9 8 7 6 5 4 3 2 1

POCKET and colophon are trademarks of Simon & Schuster.

Printed in the U.S.A.

To
Kirk and Faith Sale
and
Harrison and Sandra Starr

Contents

Sadness

Critique de la Vie Quotidienne

While I read the *Journal of Sensory Deprivation,*
Wanda, my former wife, read *Elle. Elle* was an incite-
ment to revolt to one who had majored in French in
college and had now nothing much to do with herself
except take care of a child and look out of the window.
Wanda empathized with the magazine. *"Femmes en-
ceintes, ne mangez pas de bifteck cru!" Elle* once
proclaimed, and Wanda complied. Not a shred of
bifteck cru passed her lips during the whole period of
her pregnancy. She cultivated, as *Elle* instructed, *un
petit air naïf,* or the schoolgirl look. She was always
pointing out to me four-color photographs of some
handsome restored mill in Brittany which had been
redone with Arne Jacobsen furniture and bright red and
orange plastic things from Milan: *"Une Maison Qui
Capte la Nature."* During this period *Elle* ran something like four thousand separate *actualité* pieces on

Anna Karina, the film star, and Wanda actually came to resemble her somewhat.

Our evenings lacked promise. The world in the evening seems fraught with the absence of promise, if you are a married man. There is nothing to do but go home and drink your nine drinks and forget about it.

Slumped there in your favorite chair, with your nine drinks lined up on the side table in soldierly array, and your hand never far from them, and your other hand holding on to the plump belly of the overfed child, and perhaps rocking a bit, if the chair is a rocking chair as mine was in those days, then it is true that a tiny tendril of contempt—strike that, *content*—might curl up from the storehouse where the world's content is kept, and reach into your softened brain and take hold there, persuading you that this, at last, is the fruit of all your labors, which you'd been wondering about in some such terms as, "Where is the fruit?" And so, newly cheered and warmed by this false insight, you reach out with your free hand (the one that is not clutching the nine drinks) and pat the hair of the child, and the child looks up into your face, gauging your mood as it were, and says, "Can I have a horse?", which is after all a perfectly reasonable request, in some ways, but in other ways is total ruin to that state of six-o'clock equilibrium you have so painfully achieved, because it, the child's request, is of course absolutely out of the question, and so you say "No!" as forcefully as possible—a bark rather like a bite—in such a way as to put the quietus on this project, having a horse, once and for all, permanently. But, placing yourself in the child's ragged shoes, which look more like used Brillo pads than shoes now that you regard them closely, you remember that time long ago on the other side of the Great War when you too desired a horse, and so, pulling yourself together, and putting another drink in your mouth (that makes three, I believe), you assume a thoughtful look (indeed, the same grave and thoughtful look you have been wearing all day, to confuse your enemies and armor yourself against the indifference of your friends) and begin to speak to the child softly, gently, cunningly even, explaining that the genus horse prefers the great open voids, where it can roam, and graze, and copulate with other attractive horses, to the confined space of a broke-down brownstone apartment, and that a horse if obtained would not be happy here, in the child's apartment, and does he, the child, want an unhappy horse, moping and brooding, and lying all over the double bed in the bedroom, and perhaps vomiting at intervals, and maybe even kicking down a wall or two, to express its rage? But the child, sensing the way the discussion is trending, says impatiently, with a chop of its tiny little hand, "No, I don't *mean* that," giving you to understand that it, the child, had not intended what you are arguing against but had intended something else altogether: a horse personally owned by it, the child, but pastured at a stable in the park, a horse such as Otto has—"Otto has a horse?" you say in astonishment— Otto being a school-fellow of the child, and indeed the same age, and no brighter as far as the naked eye can determine but perhaps a shade more fortunate in the wealth dimension, and the child nods, yes, Otto has a horse, and a film of tears is squeezed out and presented to you, over its eyes, and with liberal amounts of anathematization for Otto's feckless parents and the profound hope that the fall of the market has ruined them beyond repair you push the weeping child with its filmic tears off your lap and onto the floor and turn to your wife, who has been listening to all of this with her face turned to the wall, and no doubt a look upon her face corresponding to that which St. Catherine of Siena bent upon poor Pope Gregory whilst reproaching him for the luxury of Avignon, if you could see it (but of course you cannot, as her face is turned to the wall)— you look, as I say, to your wife, as the cocktail hour fades, there being only two drinks left of the nine (and you have sworn a mighty oath never to take more than nine before supper, because of what it does to you), and inquire in the calmest tones available what is for supper and would she like to take a flying fuck at the moon for visiting this outrageous child upon you. She, rising with a regal sweep of her *air naïf,* and not failing to let you have a good look at her handsome legs, those legs you could have, if you were good, motors out of the room and into the kitchen, where she throws the dinner on the floor, so that when you enter the kitchen to get some more ice you begin skidding and skating about in a muck of pork chops, squash, *sauce diable,* Danish stainless-steel flatware, and Louis Martini Mountain Red. So, this being the content of your happy hour, you decide to break your iron-clad rule, that rule of rules, and have eleven drinks instead of the modest nine with which you had been wont to stave off the song of twilight, when the lights are low, and the flickering shadows, etc., etc. But, opening the refrigerator, you discover that the slovenly bitch has failed to fill up the ice trays so there is *no more ice* for your tenth and eleventh sloshes. On discovering this you are just about ready to throw in the entire enterprise, happy home, and go to the bordel for the evening, where at least you can be sure that everyone will be kind to you, and not ask you for a horse, and the floor will not be a muck of *sauce diable* and pork chops. But when you put your hand in your pocket and discover that there are only three dollars there—not enough to cover a sortie to the bordel, where Uni-Cards are not accepted, so that the entire scheme, going to the bordel, is blasted. Upon making these determinations, which are not such as to bring the hot flush of excitement to the old cheek, you measure out your iceless over-the-limit drinks, using a little cold water as a make-do, and return to what is called the "living" room, and prepare to live, for a little while longer, in a truce with your circumstances—aware that there are wretches worse off than you, people whose trepanations have not been successful, girls who have not been invited to the sexual revolution, priests still frocked. It is seven-thirty.

I remember once we were sleeping in a narrow bed, Wanda and I, in a hotel, on a holiday, and the child crept into bed with us.

"If you insist on overburdening the bed," we said, "you must sleep at the bottom, with the feet." "But I don't want to sleep with the feet," the child said. "Sleep with the feet," we said, "they won't hurt you." "The feet kick," the child said, "in the middle of the night." "The feet or the floor," we said. "Take your choice." "Why can't I sleep with the heads," the child asked, "like everybody else?" "Because you are a child," we said, and the child subsided, whimpering, the final arguments in the case having been presented and the verdict in. But in truth the child was not without recourse; it urinated in the bed, in the vicinity of the feet. "God damn it," I said, inventing this formulation at the instant of need. "What the devil is happening, at the bottom of the bed?" "I couldn't help it," the child said. "It just came out." "I forgot to bring the plastic sheet," Wanda said. "Holy hell," I said. "Is there to be no end to this *family life?*"

I spoke to the child and the child spoke to me and the merest pleasantry trembled with enough animus to bring down an elephant.

"Clean your face," I said to the child. "It's dirty." "It's not," the child said. "By God it is," I said, "filth adheres in nine areas which I shall enumerate." "That is because of the dough," the child said. "We were taking death masks." "Dough!" I exclaimed, shocked at the idea that the child had wasted flour and water and no doubt paper too in this lightsome pastime, taking death masks. "Death!" I exclaimed for added emphasis. "What do you know of death?" "It is the end of the world," the child said, "for the death-visited individual. The world ends," the child said, "when you turn out your eyes." This was true, I could not dispute it. I returned to the main point. "Your father is telling you to wash your face," I said, locating myself in the abstract where I was more comfortable. "I know that," the child said, "that's what you always say." "Where are they, the masks?" I asked. "Drying," the child said, "on the heaterator"—its word for radiator. I then went to the place where the heaterator stood and looked. Sure enough, four tiny life masks. My child and three of its tiny friends lay there, grinning. "Who taught you how to do this?" I asked, and the child said, "We learned it in school." I cursed the school then, in my mind. "Well, what will you do with them?" I asked, demonstrating an interest in childish projects. "Hang them on the wall?" the child suggested. "Yes yes, hang them on the wall, why not?" I said. "Intimations of mortality," the child said, with a sly look. "Why the look?" I asked. "What is that supposed to mean?" "Ho ho," the child said, sniggering—a palpable snigger. "Why the snigger?" I asked, for the look in combination with the snigger had struck fear into my heart, a place where no more fear was needed. "You'll find out," the child said, testing the masks with a dirty finger to determine if they had dried. "I'll find out!" I exclaimed. "What does that mean, I'll find out!" "You'll be sorry," the child said, with a piteous glance at itself, in the mirror. But I was ahead of him there, I was already sorry. "Sorry!" I cried, "I've been sorry all my life!" "Not without reason," the child said, a wise look replacing the piteous look. I am afraid that a certain amount of physical abuse of the child ensued. But I shall not recount it, because of the shame.

"You can have the seven years," I said to Wanda. "What seven years?" Wanda asked. "The seven years by which you will, statistically, outlive me," I said. "Those years will be yours, to do with as you wish. Not a word of reproof or critique will you hear from me, during those years. I promise." "I cannot wait," Wanda said.

The child was singing. The problem was, how to make the child stop singing. It was not enough to say, "Stop singing, child!" Such saying had little effect. The child sang on despite my black look. It was characteristic of the child's singing that it was not well done. The tune went everywhere—into unexpected places on the staff, into agonies of uncertainty, into infelicities of every kind, exacerbating (left to right) the helix, the fossa of the antihelix, the antihelix, the concha, the antitragus, the tragus, the lobe, the external auditory meatus, the tympanic membrane, the malleus, the incus, the tympanum, the stapes, the Eustachian tube, the semicircular canals, the vestibule, the cochlea, the auditory nerve, the internal auditory meatus—a piercement, in fine, that God Himself would not have believed possible when He invented His great invention, the ear. "Child," I said to the child, "if you don't stop singing I will sew up your mouth, with your mother's sewing machine." "Faugh!" the child said, "you know she can't abide you." This was the living truth. The child's mother continued gazing out of the window and sucking her thumb, during this exchange. The child continued to sing and in addition turned on the television set and the transistor radio.

I remember Wanda in the morning. Up in the morning reading the *Times* I was walked past by Wanda, already sighing although not thirty seconds out of bed. At night I drank and my hostility came roaring out of its cave like a jet-assisted banshee. When we played checkers I'd glare at her so hotly she'd often miss a triple jump.

I remember that I fixed the child's bicycle, once. That brought me congratulations, around the fireside. That was a good, a fatherly thing to do. It was a cheap bicycle, $29.95 or some such, and the seat wobbled and the mother came home from the park with the bicycle in an absolute fury because the child was being penalized by my penury, in the matter of the seat. "I will fix it," I said. I went to the hardware store and bought a two-and-one-half-inch piece of pipe which I used as a collar around the seat's stem to accommodate the downward thrust. Then I affixed a flexible metal strap eight inches in length first to the back of the seat and then to the chief upright, by means of screws. This precluded side-to-side motion of the seat. A triumph of field expediency. Everyone was loving and kind that night. The child brought me my nine drinks very prettily, setting them on the side table and lining them up with the aid of a meterstick, into a perfect straight line. "Thank you," I said. We beamed at each other contesting as to who could maintain the beam the longest.

I visited the child's nursery school, once. Fathers were invited seriatim, one father a day. I sat there on a little chair while the children ran to and fro and made sport. I was served a little cake. A tiny child not my own attached herself to me. Her father was in England, she said. She had visited him there and his apartment was full of cockroaches. I wanted to take her home with me.

After the separation, which came about after what is known as the breaking point was reached, Wanda visited me in my bachelor setup. We were drinking healths. "Health to the child!" I proposed. Wanda lifted her glass. "Health to your projects!" she proposed, and I was pleased. That seemed very decent of her. I lifted my glass. The only thing I enjoy more than lifting my glass is lifting the cork, on a new bottle. I lifted the cork on a new bottle. "Health to the republic!" I proposed. We drank to that. Then Wanda proposed a health. "Health to abandoned wives!" she said. "Well now," I said. " 'Abandoned,' that's a little strong." "Pushed out, jettisoned, abjured, thrown away," she said. "I remember," I said, "a degree of mutuality, in our parting." "And when guests came," she said, "you always made me sit in the kitchen." "I thought you liked it in the kitchen," I said. "You were forever telling me to get out of the bloody kitchen." "And when my overbite required correction," she said, "you would not pay for the apparatus." "Seven years of sitting by the window with your thumb in your mouth," I said. "What did you expect?" "And when I needed a new frock," she said, "you hid the Uni-Card." "There was nothing wrong with the old one," I said, "that a few well-placed patches couldn't have fixed." "And when we were invited to the Argentine Embassy," she said, "you made me drive the car in a chauffeur's cap, and park the car, and stand about with the other drivers outside while you chatted up the Ambassador." "You know no Spanish," I pointed out. "It was not the happiest of marriages," she said, "all in all." "There has been a sixty percent increase in single-person households in the last ten years, according to the Bureau of the Census," I told her. "Perhaps we are part of a trend." That thought did not seem to console her much. "Health to the child!" I proposed, and she said, "We've already done that." "Health to the mother of the child!" I said, and she said, "I'll drink to that." To tell the truth we were getting a little wobbly on our pins, at this point. "It is probably not necessary to rise each time," I said, and she said, "Thank God," and sat. I looked at her then to see if I could discern traces of what I had seen in the beginning. There were traces but only traces. Vestiges. Hints of a formerly intact mystery never to be returned to its original wholeness. "I know what you're doing," she said, "you are touring the ruins." "Not at all," I said. "You look very well, considering." " 'Considering'!" she cried, and withdrew from her bosom an extremely large horse pistol. "Health to the dead!" she proposed, meanwhile waving the horse pistol in the air in an agitated manner. I drank that health, but with misgivings, because who was she talking about? "The sacred dead," she said with relish. "The well-beloved, the well-esteemed, the well-remembered, the well-ventilated." She attempted to ventilate me then, with the horse pistol. The barrel wavered to the right of my head, and to the left of my head, and I remembered that although its guidance system was primitive its caliber was large. The weapon discharged with a blurt of sound and the ball smashed a bottle of J & B on the mantel. She wept. The place stank of Scotch. I called her a cab.

Wanda is happier now, I think. She has taken herself off to Nanterre, where she is studying Marxist sociology with Lefebvre (not impertinently, the author of the *Critique de la Vie Quotidienne*). The child is being cared for in an experimental nursery school for the children of graduate students run, I understand, in accord with the best Piagetian principles. And I, I have my J & B. The J & B company keeps manufacturing it, case after case, year in and year out, and there is, I am told, no immediate danger of a dearth.

Träumerei

So there you are, Daniel, reclining, reclining on the chaise, a lovely picture, white trousers, white shirt, red cummerbund, scarlet rather, white suède jacket, sunflower in buttonhole, beard neatly combed, let's have a look at the fingernails. Daniel, your fingernails are a disgrace. Have a herring. We are hungry, Daniel, we could eat the hind leg off a donkey. Quickly, Daniel, quickly to the bath, it's time to bathe, the bath is drawn, the towels laid out, the soap in the soap dish, the new bath mat laid down, the bust of Puccini over the tub polished, the choir is ready, it will sing the *Nelson Mass* of Haydn, soaping to begin with the Kyrie, luxuriating from the Kyrie to the Credo, serious scrubbing from the Credo to the Sanctus, toweling to commence with the Agnus Dei. Daniel, walk the dog and frighten the birds, we can't abide birdsong. Spontini is eternal, Daniel, we knew him well, he sat often in that very chair, the chair you sit in, Spontini sat there, hawking and spitting, coughing blood into a plaid handkerchief, he was not in the best of health after he left Berlin, we were very close, Daniel, Spontini and we, *Agnes von Hohenstaufen* was his favorite among his works, "not lacking in historical significance," he used to say of it, in his modest way, and of course he was right, *Agnes von Hohenstaufen* is eternal. Daniel, do you know a Putzi, no Putzi appears in the register, what is this, Daniel, a new Putzi and not recorded in the register, what marches, are you conducting a little fiddle here, Daniel, Putzi is on the telephone, hurry to the telephone, Daniel. Daniel, you may begin bringing in the sheaves. Do you want *all* the herring, Daniel? For a day, Daniel, we sat before a Constable sketch in a dream, an entire day, twenty-four hours, the light failed and we had candles brought, we cried "Ho! Candles, this way, lights, lights, lights!" and candles were brought, and we gazed additionally, some additional gazes, at the Constable sketch, in a dream. Have a shot of aquavit, Daniel. And there's an old croquet ball! It's been so long since we've played, almost forgotten how, perhaps some evening in the cool, while the light lasts, we'll have a game, we were very apt once, probably you are not, but we'll teach you, pure pleasure, Daniel, pure and unrestricted pleasure, while the light lasts, indulgence at its fiery height, you will lust after the last wicket, you will rush for the stake, and miss it, very likely, the untutored amateur in his eagerness, you'll be hit off into the shrubbery, we will place our ball next to your ball, and place a foot on your ball, and give it a good whack, your ball will go flying off into the shrubbery, what a pleasure, it frightens the birds. That is our croquet elegy, Daniel. Repair the dog cart, Daniel. Or have another herring, we were ripping up a herring with

Mascagni once, some decades ago, the eternal Mascagni, a wonderful man, Pietro, a great laugher, he would laugh and laugh, and then stop laughing, and grow gray, a disappointed man, Pietro, brought a certain amount of grayness into one's drawing room, relieved of course by the laughing, from time to time, he was a rocket, Mascagni, worldwide plaudits and then pop! nothing, not a plaudit in a carload, he grew a bit morose, in his last years, and gray, perhaps that's usual when one's plaudits have been taken away, a darling man, and wonderful with the stick, always on the road in his last years, opera orchestras, he was the devil with your work-shy element, was Pietro, your work-shy element might as well bend to it when Pietro was in the pit. You may go to your room now, Daniel. She loves you still, we can't understand it, they all profess an unexhausted passion, the whole string, that's remarkable, Putzi too, you're to be congratulated and we are never the last to offer our congratulations, the persistence of memory as the poet puts it, would that be the case do you think, would that be the explanation, hurry to the cellar and bring up a cask of herring and four bottles of aquavit, we're going to let you work on the wall. We had a man working on the wall, Daniel, a good man, Buller by name, knew his trade, did Buller, but he went away, to the West, an offer from the Corps of Engineers, they were straightening a river, somewhere in the West, Buller had straightened streams in his youth but never a river, he couldn't resist, gave us a turkey by way of farewell, it was that season, we gave him a watch, inscribed TO BULLER, FAITHFUL POURER OF FOOTINGS, and then he hove out of view, hove over the horizon, run to the wall, Daniel, you'll find the concrete block stacked on the site, and mind your grout, Daniel, mind your grout. Daniel, you're looking itchy, we know that itch, we are not insensible of your problem, in our youth we whored after youth, on the one hand, and whored after beauty, on the other, very often these were combined in the same object, a young girl for example, a simplification, one does not have to whore after youth and whore after beauty consecutively, running first to the left, down dark streets, whoring after youth, and then to the right, through the arcades, whoring after beauty, and generally whoring oneself ragged, please, Daniel, don't do that, throwing the cat against the wall *injures the cat*. Your women, Daniel, have arrayed themselves on the garden gate. There's a racket down at the garden gate, Daniel, see to it, and the damned birds singing, and think for a while about delayed gratification, it's what distinguishes us from the printed circuits, Daniel, your printed circuit can't delay a gratification worth a damn. Daniel, run and buy a barrel of herring from the herringvolk. For we deny no man his mead, after a hard day at the wall. Your grout is lovely, Daniel. Daniel, have you noticed this herring, it looks very much like the President, do you think so, we are soliciting your opinion, although we are aware that most people think the President looks not like a herring but like a foot, what is your opinion, Daniel. Glazunov is eternal, of course, eight symphonies, two piano concertos, a violin concerto, a cello concerto, a concerto for saxophone, six overtures, seven quartets, a symphonic poem, serenades, fantasias, incidental music, and the Hymn to Pushkin. Pass the aquavit, Daniel. There was a moment when we thought we were losing our mind. Yes, we, losing our mind, the wall not even started at that period, we were open to the opinions of mankind, vulnerable, anyone could come along, as you did, Daniel, and have an opinion contrary to our opinion, we remember when the

Monsignor came to inspect our miracle, a wonderful little miracle that had happened to us, still believers, at that period, we had the exhibits spread out on the rug, neatly tagged, Exhibit A, Exhibit B, and so forth, the Monsignor tickled the exhibits with his toe, toed the exhibits reflectively, or perhaps he was merely trying to give that impression, they're cunning, you never know, we had prostrated ourselves of course, then he tickled the tops of our heads with his toe and said, "Get up, you fools, get up and pour me a glass of that sherry I spy there, on the sideboard," we got up and poured him a glass, with trembling hands you may be sure, and the damned birds singing, he sipped, a smile appeared on the monsignorial mug, "Well boys," he said, "a few cases of this spread around the chancellery won't do your petition any harm," we immediately went to the cellar, loaded six cases upon a dray and caused them to be drayed to the chancellery, but to no avail, spurious they said, of our miracle, we were crushed, blasted, we thought we were losing our mind. You, Daniel, can be the new miracle, in your white trousers, white suède jacket, red cummerbund, scarlet rather, yellow sunflower in the bottonhole, a miracle of nullity, pass the aquavit. Have a reindeer steak, Daniel, it's Dancer, Dancer or Prancer, no no, that's a joke, Daniel, and while you're at it bring the accounts, your pocket money must be accounted for, thirty-five cents a week times thirteen weeks, what? Thirty-five cents a week times twenty-six weeks, we did not realize that your option had been picked up, you will be the comfort of our old age, Daniel, if you live. Give the herb garden a weed, Daniel. The telephone is ringing, Daniel, answer it, we'll be here, sipping hock and listening on the extensions. Your backing and filling, your excuses, their reproaches, the weeping, all very well in a way, stimulating even, but it palls, your palaver, after a time, these ladies, poor girls, the whole string, Martha, Mary, all the rest, Claudia or is it Claudine, we can't remember, amusing, yes, for a time, for a time, until the wall is completed, a perfect circle or is it a perfect rhomboid, we can't remember. We remember browsing in the dictionary, page something or other, pumpernickel to puppyish, keeping the mind occupied, until the wall is completed, young whelp, what are you now, thirty-eight, thirty-nine, almost a neonate, have a herring, and count your blessings, and mind your grout, and give the fingernails a buff, spurious they said, of our miracle, that was a downer, and the damned birds singing, we're spared nothing, and the cat with its head cracked, thanks to you, Daniel, the garden gate sprung, thanks to you, Daniel, Mascagni gone, Glazunov gone, and the damned birds singing, and the croquet balls God knows where, and the damned birds singing.

The Genius

His assistants cluster about him. He is severe with them, demanding, punctilious, but this is for their own ultimate benefit. He devises hideously difficult problems, or complicates their work with sudden oblique comments that open whole new areas of investigation—yawning chasms under their feet. It is as if he wishes to place them in situations where only failure is possible. But failure, too, is a part of mental life. "I will make you failure-proof," he says jokingly. His assistants pale.

•

Is it true, as Valéry said, that every man of genius contains within himself a false man of genius?

•

"This is an age of personal ignorance. No one knows what others know. No one knows enough."

•

The genius is afraid to fly. The giant aircraft seem to him . . . *flimsy*. He hates the takeoff and he hates the landing and he detests being in the air. He hates the food, the stewardesses, the voice of the captain, and his fellow-passengers, especially those who are conspicuously at ease, who remove their coats, loosen their ties, and move up and down the aisles with drinks in their hands. In consequence, he rarely travels. The world comes to him.

•

Q: What do you consider the most important tool of the genius of today?
A: Rubber cement.

•

He has urged that America be divided into four smaller countries. America, he says, is too big. "America does not look where it puts its foot," he says. This comment, which, coming from anyone else, would have engendered widespread indignation, is greeted with amused chuckles. The Chamber of Commerce sends him four cases of Teacher's Highland Cream.

•

The genius defines "inappropriate response":
"Suppose my friend telephones and asks, 'Is my wife there?' 'No,' I reply, 'they went out, your wife and my

wife, wearing new hats, they are giving themselves to sailors.' My friend is astounded at this news. 'But it's Election Day!' he cries. 'And it's beginning to rain!' I say.''

The genius pays close attention to work being done in fields other than his own. He is well read in all of the sciences (with the exception of the social sciences); he follows the arts with a connoisseur's acuteness; he is an accomplished amateur musician. He jogs. He dislikes chess. He was once photographed playing tennis with the Marx Brothers.

He has devoted considerable thought to an attempt to define the sources of his genius. However, this attempt has led approximately nowhere. The mystery remains a mystery. He has therefore settled upon the following formula, which he repeats each time he is interviewed: ''Historical forces.''

•

The government has decided to award the genius a few new medals—medals he has not been previously awarded. One medal is awarded for his work prior to 1936, one for his work from 1936 to the present, and one for his future work.

•

''I think that this thing, my work, has made me, in a sense, what I am. The work possesses a consciousness which shapes that of the worker. The work flatters the worker. Only the strongest worker can do this work, the work says. You must be a fine fellow, that you can do this work. But disaffection is also possible. The worker grows careless. The worker pays slight regard to the work, he ignores the work, he flirts with other work, he is *unfaithful* to the work. The work is insulted. And perhaps it finds little ways of telling the worker . . . The work slips in the hands of the worker—a little cut on the finger. You understand? The work becomes slow, sulky, consumes more time, becomes more tiring. The gaiety that once existed between the worker and the work has evaporated. A fine situation! Don't you think?''

●

The genius has noticed that he does not interact with children successfully. (Anecdote)

●

Richness of the inner life of the genius:

(1) Manic-oceanic states
(2) Hatred of children
(3) Piano playing
(4) Subincised genitals
(5) Subscription to *Harper's Bazaar*
(6) Stamp collection

●

The genius receives a very flattering letter from the University of Minnesota. The university wishes to become the depository of his papers, after he is dead. A new wing of the Library will be built to house them.

The letter makes the genius angry. He takes a pair of scissors, cuts the letter into long thin strips, and mails it back to the Director of Libraries.

●

He takes long walks through the city streets, noting architectural details—particularly old ironwork. His mind is filled with ideas for a new— But at this moment a policeman approaches him. "Beg pardon, sir. Aren't you—" "Yes," the genius says, smiling. "My little boy is an admirer of yours," the policeman says. He pulls out a pocket notebook. "If it's not too much trouble . . ." Smiling, the genius signs his name.

The genius carries his most important papers about with him in a green Sears, Roebuck toolbox.

•

He did not win the Nobel Prize again this year.

It was neither the year of his country nor the year of his discipline. To console him, the National Foundation gives him a new house.

•

The genius meets with a group of students. The students tell the genius that the concept "genius" is not, currently, a popular one. Group effort, they say, is more socially productive than the isolated efforts of any one man, however gifted. Genius by its very nature sets itself over against the needs of the many. In answering its own imperatives, genius tends toward, even embraces, totalitarian forms of social organization. Tyranny of the gifted over the group, while bringing some advances in the short run, inevitably produces a set of conditions which—

The genius smokes thoughtfully.

•

A giant brown pantechnicon disgorges the complete works of the Venerable Bede, in all translations, upon the genius's lawn—a gift from the people of Cincinnati!

•

The genius is leafing through a magazine. Suddenly he is arrested by an advertisement:

> WHY DON'T YOU
> BECOME A
> PROFESSIONAL
> INTERIOR DECORATOR?

Interior decoration is a high-income field, the advertisement says. The work is varied and interesting. One moves in a world of fashion, creativity, and ever-new challenge.

The genius tears out the advertisement's coupon.

•

Q: Is America a good place for genius?
A: I have found America most hospitable to genius.

•

"I always say to myself, 'What is the most important thing I can be thinking about at this minute?' But then I don't think about it."

•

His driver's license expires. But he does nothing about renewing it. He is vaguely troubled by the thought of the expired license (although he does not stop driving). But he loathes the idea of taking the examination again, of going physically to the examining station, of waiting in line for an examiner. He decides that if he writes a letter to the License Bureau requesting a new license, the bureau will grant him one without an examination, because he is a genius. He is right. He writes the letter and the License Bureau sends him a new license, by return mail.

•

In the serenity of his genius, the genius reaches out to right wrongs—the sewer systems of cities, for example.

•

The genius is reading *The Genius,* a 736-page novel by Theodore Dreiser. He arrives at the last page:

". . . What a sweet welter life is—how rich, how tender, how grim, how like a colorful symphony."
Great art dreams welled up into his soul as he viewed the sparkling deeps of space . . .

The genius gets up and looks at himself in a mirror.

•

An organization has been formed to appreciate his thought: the Blaufox Gesellschaft. Meetings are held once a month, in a room over a cafeteria in Buffalo, New York. He has always refused to have anything to do with the Gesellschaft, which reminds him uncomfortably of the Browning Society. However, he cannot prevent himself from glancing at the group's twice-yearly *Proceedings,* which contains such sentences as "The imbuement of all reaches of the scholarly community with Blaufox's views must, *ab ovo,* be our . . ."

He falls into hysteria.

•

Moments of self-doubt . . .
"Am I really a—"
"What does it *mean* to be a—"
"Can one *refuse* to be a—"

•

His worse moment: He is in a church, kneeling in a pew near the back. He is gradually made aware of a row of nuns, a half dozen, kneeling twenty feet ahead of him, their heads bent over their beads. One of the nuns however has turned her head almost completely around, and seems to be staring at him. The genius glances at her, glances away, then looks again: she is still staring at him. The genius is only visiting the church in the first place because the nave is said to be a particularly fine example of Burgundian Gothic. He places his eyes here, there, on the altar, on the stained glass, but each time they return to the nuns, *his* nun is still staring. The genius says to himself, *This is my worst moment.*

•

He is a drunk.

•

"A truly potent abstract concept avoids, resists closure. The ragged, blurred outlines of such a concept, like a net in which the fish have eaten large, gaping holes, permit entry and escape equally. What does one catch in such a net? The sea horse with a Monet in his mouth. How did the Monet get there? Is the value of the Monet less because it has gotten wet? Are there tooth marks in the Monet? Do sea horses have teeth? How large is the Monet? From which period? Is it a water lily or group of water lilies? Do sea horses eat water lilies? Does Parke-Bernet know? Do oil and water mix? Is a mixture of oil and water bad for the digestion of the sea horse? Should art be expensive? Should artists wear beards? Ought beards to be forbidden by law? Is underwater art better than overwater art? What does the expression 'glad rags' mean? Does it refer to Monet's paint rags? In the Paris of 1878, what was the average monthly rent for a north-lit, spacious studio in an unfashionable district? If sea horses eat water lilies, what percent of their daily work energy, expressed in ergs, is generated thereby? Should the holes in the net be mended? In a fight between a sea horse and a flittermouse, which would you bet on? If I mend the net, will you forgive me? Do water rats chew upon the water lilies? Is there a water buffalo in the water cooler? If I fill my water gun to the waterline, can I then visit the watering place? Is fantasy an adequate substitute for correct behavior?''

•

The genius proposes a world inventory of genius, in order to harness and coordinate the efforts of genius everywhere to create a better life for all men.

Letters are sent out . . .

The response is staggering!

Telegrams pour in . . .

Geniuses of every stripe offer their cooperation.
The *Times* prints an editorial praising the idea . . .
Three thousand geniuses in one room!
    The genius falls into an ill humor. He refuses to speak
to anyone for eight days.

•

But now a green Railway Express truck arrives at his
door. It contains a field of stainless-steel tulips, courtesy of the Mayor and City Council of Houston, Texas.
The genius signs the receipt, smiling . . .

Perpetua

1.

Now Perpetua was living alone. She had told her husband that she didn't want to live with him any longer.

"Why not?" he had asked.

"For all the reasons you know," she said.

Harold's farewell gift was a Blue Cross-Blue Shield insurance policy, paid up for one year. Now Perpetua was putting valve oil on her trumpet. One of the valves was sticking. She was fourth-chair trumpet with the New World Symphony Orchestra.

Perpetua thought: That time he banged the car door on my finger. I am sure it was deliberate. That time he locked me out while I was pregnant and I had to walk four miles after midnight to my father's house. One does not forget.

Perpetua smiled at the new life she saw spread out before her like a red velvet map.

Back in the former house, Harold watched television.

Perpetua remembered the year she was five. She had to learn to be nice, all in one year. She only learned part of it. She was not fully nice until she was seven.

Now I must obtain a lover, she thought. Perhaps more than one. One for Monday, one for Tuesday, one for Wednesday . . .

2.

Harold was looking at a picture of the back of a naked girl, in a magazine for men. The girl was pulling a dress over her head, in the picture. This girl has a nice-looking back, Harold thought. I wonder where she lives?

Perpetua sat on the couch in her new apartment smoking dope with a handsome bassoon player. A few cats walked around.

"Our art contributes nothing to the revolution," the bassoon player said. "We cosmeticize reality."

"We are trustees of Form," Perpetua said.

"It is hard to make the revolution with a bassoon," the bassoon player said.

"Sabotage?" Perpetua suggested.

"Sabotage would get me fired," her companion replied. "The sabotage would be confused with ineptness anyway."

I am tired of talking about the revolution, Perpetua thought.

"Go away," she said. The bassoon player put on his black raincoat and left.

It is wonderful to be able to tell them to go away, she reflected. Then she said aloud, "Go away. Go away. Go away."

Harold went to visit his child, Peter. Peter was at

school in New England. "How do you like school?"
Harold asked Peter.

"It's O.K.," Peter said. "Do you have a light?"

Harold and Peter watched the game together. Peter's
school won. After the game, Harold went home.

3.

Perpetua went to her mother's house for Christmas.
Her mother was cooking the eighty-seventh turkey of
her life. "God damn this turkey!" Perpetua's mother
shouted. "If anyone knew how I hate, loathe, and
despise turkeys. If I had known that I would cook
eighty-seven separate and distinct turkeys in my life, I
would have split forty-four years ago. I would have
been long gone for the tall timber."

Perpetua's mother showed her a handsome new
leather coat. "Tanned in the bile of matricides," her
mother said, with a meaningful look.

Harold wrote to the magazine for men asking for the
name and address of the girl whose back had bewitched
him. The magazine answered his letter saying that it
could not reveal this information. The magazine was
not a pimp, it said.

Harold, enraged, wrote to the magazine and said that
if the magazine was not a pimp, what was it? The
magazine answered that while it could not in all con-
science give Harold the girl's address, it would be glad
to give him her grid coordinates. Harold, who had had
map reading in the Army, was delighted.

4.

Perpetua sat in the trumpet section of the New World
Symphony Orchestra. She had a good view of the other

players because the sections were on risers and the
trumpet section sat on the highest riser of all. They were
playing Brahms. A percussionist had just split a head on
the bass drum. "I luff Brahms," he explained.

Perpetua thought: I wish this so-called conductor
would get his movie together.

After the concert she took off her orchestra uniform
and put on her suède jeans, her shirt made of a lot of
colored scarves sewn together, her carved-wood neck
bracelet, and her D'Artagnan cape with its silver lining.

Perpetua could not remember what was this year and
what was last year. Had something just happened, or
had it happened a long time ago? She met many new
people. "You are different," Perpetua said to Sunny
Marge. "Very few of the girls I know wear a tattoo of
the head of Marshal Foch on their backs."

"I am different," Sunny Marge agreed. "Since I
posed for that picture in that magazine for men, many
people have been after my back. My back has become
practically an international incident. So I decided to
alter it."

"Will it come off? Ever?"

"I hope and pray."

Perpetua slept with Robert in his loft. His children
were sleeping on mattresses in the other room. It was
cold. Robert said that when he was a child he was
accused by his teacher of being "pert."

"Pert?"

Perpetua and Robert whispered to each other, on the
mattress.

5.

Perpetua said, "Now, I am alone. I have thrown my
husband away. I remember him. Once he seemed

necessary to me, or at least important, or at least interesting. Now none of these things is true. Now he is as strange to me as something in the window of a pet shop. I gaze into the pet-shop window, the Irish setters move about, making their charming moves, I see the moves and see that they are charming, yet I am not charmed. An Irish setter is what I do not need. I remember my husband awaking in the morning, inserting his penis in his penis sheath, placing ornaments of bead and feather on his upper arms, smearing his face with ochre and umber—broad lines under the eyes and across the brow. I remember him taking his blowpipe from the umbrella stand and leaving for the office. What he did there I never knew. Slew his enemies, he said. Our dinner table was decorated with the heads of his enemies, whom he had slain. It was hard to believe one man could have so many enemies. Or maybe they were the same enemies, slain over and over and over. He said he saw girls going down the street who broke his heart, in their loveliness. I no longer broke his heart, he said. I had not broken his heart for at least a year, perhaps more than a year, with my loveliness. Well screw that, I said, screw that. My oh my, he said, my oh my, what a mouth. He meant that I was foulmouthed. This, I said, is just the beginning."

In the desert, Harold's Land-Rover had a flat tire. Harold got out of the Land-Rover and looked at his map. Could this be the wrong map?

6.

Perpetua was scrubbing Sunny Marge's back with a typewriter eraser.

"Oh. Ouch. Oh. Ouch."

"I'm not making much progress," Perpetua said.

"Well I suppose it will have to be done by the passage of time," Sunny Marge said, looking at her back in the mirror.

"Years are bearing us to Heaven," Perpetua agreed.

Perpetua and Sunny Marge went cruising, on the boulevard. They saw a man coming toward them.

"He's awfully clean-looking," Perpetua said.

"Probably he's from out of town," Sunny Marge said.

Edmund was a small farmer.

"What is your cash crop?" Sunny Marge asked.

"We have two hundred acres in hops," the farmer replied. "That reminds me, would you ladies like a drink?"

"*I'd* like a drink," Perpetua said.

"I'd like a drink too," Sunny Marge said. "Do you know anywhere he can go, in those clothes?"

"Maybe we'd better go back to my place," Perpetua said.

At Perpetua's apartment Edmund recounted the history of hops.

"Would you like to see something interesting?" Sunny Marge asked Edmund.

"What is it?"

"A portrait of Marshal Foch, a French hero of World War I."

"Sure," Edmund said.

The revolution called and asked Perpetua if she would tape an album of songs of the revolution.

"Sure," Perpetua said.

Harold took ship for home. He shared a cabin with a man whose hobby was building scale models of tank battles.

"This is a *Sturmgeschütz* of the 1945 period," the man said. "Look at the bullet nicks. The bullet nicks are done by applying a small touch of gray paint with a burst effect of flat white. For small holes in the armor, I pierce with a hot nail.''

The floor of Harold's cabin was covered with tanks locked in duels to the death.

Harold hurried to the ship's bar. I wonder how Perpetua is doing, he thought. I wonder if she is happier without me. Probably she is. Probably she has found deep contentment by now. But maybe not.

7.

Perpetua met many new people. She met Henry, who was a cathedral builder. He built cathedrals in places where there were no cathedrals—Twayne, Nebraska, for example. Every American city needed a cathedral, Henry said. The role of the cathedral in the building of the national soul was well known. We should punish ourselves in our purses, Henry said, to shape up the national soul. An arch never sleeps, Henry said, pointing to the never-sleeping arches in his plans. Architecture is memory, Henry said, and the nation that had no cathedrals to speak of had no memory to speak of either. He did it all, Henry said, with a 30-man crew composed of 1 superintendent 1 masonry foreman 1 ironworker foreman 1 carpenter foreman 1 pipefitter foreman 1 electrician foreman 2 journeyman masons 2 journeyman ironworkers 2 journeyman carpenters 2 journeyman pipefitters 2 journeyman electricians 1 mason's helper 1 ironworker's helper 1 carpenter's helper 1 pipefitter's helper 1 electrician's helper 3 gargoyle carvers 1 grimer 1 clerk-of-the-works 1 master fund-raiser 2 journeyman fund-raisers and 1 fund-raiser's helper. Cathedrals are mostly a matter of thrusts, Henry said. You got to balance your thrusts.

The ribs of your vaults intersect collecting the vertical and lateral thrusts at fixed points which are then buttressed or grounded although that's not so important anymore when you use a steel skeleton as we do which may be cheating but I always say that cheating in the Lord's name is O.K. as long as He don't catch you at it. Awe and grace, Henry said, awe and grace, that's what we're selling and we offer a Poet's Corner where any folks who were poets or even suspected of being poets can be buried, just like Westminster Abbey. The financing is the problem, Henry said. What we usually do is pick out some old piece of ground that was a cornfield or something like that, and put it in the Soil Bank. We take that piece of ground out of production and promise the government we won't grow no more corn on it no matter how they beg and plead with us. Well the government sends a man around from the Agriculture Department and he agrees with us that there certainly ain't no corn growing there. So we ask him about how much he thinks we can get from the Soil Bank and he says it looks like around a hundred and fifty thousand a year to him but that he will have to check with the home office and we can't expect the money before around the middle of next week. We tell him that will be fine and we all go have a drink over to the Holiday Inn. Of course the hundred and fifty thousand is just a spit in the ocean but it pays for the four-color brochures. By this time we got our artist's rendering of the Twayne Undenominational Cathedral sitting right in the lobby of the Valley National Bank on a card table covered with angel hair left over from Christmas, and the money is just pouring in. And I'm worrying about how we're going to *staff* this cathedral. We need a sexton and a bellringer and a beadle and maybe an undenominational archbishop, and that last is hard to come by. Pretty soon the ground is broken and the steel is up, and the Bell Committee is wrangling about whether the carillon is going to be sixteen bells or thirty-two. There is something about cathedral building that men like, Henry said, this has often been noticed. And the first thing you know it's Dedication Day and the whole state is there, it seems like, with long lines of little girls carrying bouquets of mistflowers and the Elks Honor Guard presenting arms with M-16s sent back in pieces from Nam and reassembled for domestic use, and the band is playing the Albinoni Adagio in G Minor which is the saddest piece of music ever written by mortal man and the light is streaming through the guaranteed stained-glass windows and the awe is so thick you could cut it with a knife.

"You are something else, Henry," Perpetua said.

8.

Perpetua and André went over to have dinner with Sunny Marge and Edmund.

"This is André," Perpetua said.

André, a well-dressed graduate of the École du Regard, managed a large industry in Reims.

Americans were very strange, André said. They did not have a stable pattern of family life, as the French did. This was attributable to the greater liberty— perhaps license was not too strong a term—permitted to American women by their husbands and lovers. American women did not know where their own best interests lay, André said. The intoxication of modern life, which was in part a result of the falling away of former standards of conduct . . .

Perpetua picked up a chicken leg and tucked it into the breast pocket of André's coat.

"Goodbye, André."

Peter called Perpetua from his school in New England.

"What's the matter, Peter?"

"I'm lonesome."

"Do you want to come stay with me for a while?"

"No. Can you send me fifty dollars?"

"Yes. What do you want it for?"

"I want to buy some blue racers."

Peter collected snakes. Sometimes Perpetua thought that the snakes were dearer to him than she was.

9.

Harold walked into Perpetua's apartment.

"Harold," Perpetua said.

"I just want to ask you one question," Harold said. "Are you happier now than you were before?"

"Sure," Perpetua said.

A City of Churches

"Yes," Mr. Phillips said, "ours is a city of churches all right."

Cecelia nodded, following his pointing hand. Both sides of the street were solidly lined with churches, standing shoulder to shoulder in a variety of architectural styles. The Bethel Baptist stood next to the Holy Messiah Free Baptist, St. Paul's Episcopal next to Grace Evangelical Covenant. Then came the First Christian Science, the Church of God, All Souls, Our Lady of Victory, the Society of Friends, the Assembly of God, and the Church of the Holy Apostles. The spires and steeples of the traditional buildings were jammed in next to the broad imaginative flights of the "contemporary" designs.

"Everyone here takes a great interest in church matters," Mr. Phillips said.

Will I fit in? Cecelia wondered. She had come to Prester to open a branch office of a car-rental concern.

"I'm not especially religious," she said to Mr. Phillips, who was in the real-estate business.

"Not *now*," he answered. "Not *yet*. But we have many fine young people here. You'll get integrated into the community soon enough. The immediate problem is, where are you to live? Most people," he said, "live in the church of their choice. All of our churches have many extra rooms. I have a few belfry apartments that I can show you. What price range were you thinking of?"

They turned a corner and were confronted with more churches. They passed St. Luke's, the Church of the Epiphany, All Saints Ukrainian Orthodox, St. Clement's, Fountain Baptist, Union Congregational, St. Anargyri's, Temple Emanuel, the First Church of Christ Reformed. The mouths of all the churches were gaping open. Inside, lights could be seen dimly.

"I can go up to a hundred and ten," Cecelia said. "Do you have any buildings here that are *not* churches?"

"None," said Mr. Phillips. "Of course many of our fine church structures also do double duty as something else." He indicated a handsome Georgian façade. "That one," he said, "houses the United Methodist and the Board of Education. The one next to it, which is Antioch Pentecostal, has the barbershop."

It was true. A red-and-white striped barber pole was attached inconspicuously to the front of the Antioch Pentecostal.

"Do many people rent cars here?" Cecelia asked. "Or would they, if there was a handy place to rent them?"

"Oh, I don't know," said Mr. Phillips. "Renting a car implies that you want to go somewhere. Most people are pretty content right here. We have a lot of activities. I don't think I'd pick the car-rental business if I was just starting out in Prester. But you'll do fine." He showed her a small, extremely modern building with a severe brick, steel, and glass front. "That's St. Barnabas. Nice bunch of people over there. Wonderful spaghetti suppers."

Cecelia could see a number of heads looking out of the windows. But when they saw that she was staring at them, the heads disappeared.

"Do you think it's healthy for so many churches to be gathered together in one place?" she asked her guide. "It doesn't seem . . . *balanced,* if you know what I mean."

"We are famous for our churches," Mr. Phillips replied. "They are harmless. Here we are now."

He opened a door and they began climbing many flights of dusty stairs. At the end of the climb they entered a good-sized room, square, with windows on all four sides. There was a bed, a table, and two chairs, lamps, a rug. Four very large bronze bells hung in the exact center of the room.

"What a view!" Mr. Phillips exclaimed. "Come here and look."

"Do they actually ring these bells?" Cecelia asked.

"Three times a day," Mr. Phillips said, smiling. "Morning, noon, and night. Of course when they're rung you have to be pretty quick at getting out of the way. You get hit in the head by one of these babies and that's all she wrote."

"God Almighty," said Cecelia involuntarily. Then she said, "Nobody lives in the belfry apartments. That's why they're empty."

"You think so?" Mr. Phillips said.

"You can only rent them to new people in town," she said accusingly.

"I wouldn't do that," Mr. Phillips said. "It would go against the spirit of Christian fellowship."

"This town is a little creepy, you know that?"

"That may be, but it's not for you to say, is it? I mean, you're new here. You should walk cautiously, for a while. If you don't want an upper apartment I have a basement over at Central Presbyterian. You'd have to share it. There are two women in there now."

"I don't want to share," Cecelia said. "I want a place of my own."

"Why?" the real-estate man asked curiously. "For what purpose?"

"Purpose?" asked Cecelia. "There is no particular purpose. I just want—"

"That's not usual here. Most people live with other people. Husbands and wives. Sons with their mothers. People have roommates. That's the usual pattern."

"Still, I prefer a place of my own."

"It's very unusual."

"Do you have any such places? Besides bell towers, I mean?"

"I guess there are a few," Mr. Phillips said, with clear reluctance. "I can show you one or two, I suppose."

He paused for a moment.

"It's just that we have different values, maybe, from some of the surrounding communities," he explained. "We've been written up a lot. We had four minutes on the C.B.S. Evening News one time. Three or four years ago. 'A City of Churches,' it was called."

"Yes, a place of my own is essential," Cecelia said, "if I am to survive here."

"That's kind of a funny attitude to take," Mr. Phillips said. "What denomination are you?"

Cecelia was silent. The truth was, she wasn't anything.

"I said, what denomination are you?" Mr. Phillips repeated.

"I can will my dreams," Cecelia said. "I can dream whatever I want. If I want to dream that I'm having a good time, in Paris or some other city, all I have to do is go to sleep and I will dream that dream. I can dream whatever I want."

"What do you dream, then, mostly?" Mr. Phillips said, looking at her closely.

"Mostly sexual things," she said. She was not afraid of him.

"Prester is not that kind of a town," Mr. Phillips said, looking away.

They went back down the stairs.

The doors of the churches were opening, on both sides of the street. Small groups of people came out and stood there, in front of the churches, gazing at Cecelia and Mr. Phillips.

A young man stepped forward and shouted, *"Everyone in this town already has a car! There is no one in this town who doesn't have a car!"*

"Is that true?" Cecelia asked Mr. Phillips.

"Yes," he said. "It's true. No one would rent a car here. Not in a hundred years."

"Then I won't stay," she said. "I'll go somewhere else."

"You must stay," he said. "There is already a car-rental office for you. In Mount Moriah Baptist, on the lobby floor. There is a counter and a telephone and a rack of car keys. And a calendar."

"I won't stay," she said. "Not if there's not any sound business reason for staying."

"We want you," said Mr. Phillips. "We want you standing behind the counter of the car-rental agency, during regular business hours. It will make the town complete."

"I won't," she said. "Not me."

"You must. It's essential."

"I'll dream," she said. "Things you won't like."

"We are discontented," said Mr. Phillips. "Terribly, terribly discontented. Something is wrong."

"I'll dream the Secret," she said. "You'll be sorry."

"We are like other towns, except that we are perfect," he said. "Our discontent can only be held in check by perfection. We need a car-rental girl. Someone must stand behind that counter."

"I'll dream the life you are most afraid of," Cecelia threatened.

"You are ours," he said, gripping her arm. "Our car-rental girl. Be nice. There is nothing you can do."

"Wait and see," Cecelia said.

The Party

I went to a party and corrected a pronunciation. The
man whose voice I had adjusted fell back into the
kitchen. I praised a Bonnard. It was not a Bonnard. My
new glasses, I explained, and I'm terribly sorry, but
significant variations elude me, vodka exhausts me, I
was young once, essential services are being maintained. Drums, drums, drums, outside the windows. I
thought that if I could persuade you to say "No," then
my own responsibility would be limited, or changed,
another sort of life would be possible, different from the
life we had previously, somewhat skeptically, enjoyed
together. But you had wandered off into another room,
testing the effect on members of the audience of your
ruffled blouse, your long magenta skirt. Giant hands,
black, thick with fur, reaching in through the windows.
Yes, it was King Kong, back in action, and all of the
guests uttered loud exclamations of fatigue and disgust,

examining the situation in the light of their own needs and emotions, hoping that the ape was real or papier-mâché according to their temperaments, or wondering whether other excitements were possible out in the crisp, white night.

"Did you see him?"

"Let us pray."

The important tasks of a society are often entrusted to people who have fatal flaws. Of course we tried hard, it was intelligent to do so, extraordinary efforts were routine. Your zest was, and is, remarkable. But carrying over into private life attitudes that have been successful in the field of public administration is not, perhaps, a good idea. Zest is not fun for everybody. I am aware that roles change. Kong himself is now an adjunct professor of art history at Rutgers, co-author of a text on tomb sculpture; if he chooses to come to a party through the window he is simply trying to make himself interesting. A lady spoke to me, she had in her hand a bunch of cattleyas. "I have attempted to be agreeable," she said, "but it's like teaching iron to swim, with this group." Zest is not fun for everybody. When whippoorwills called, you answered. And then I would go out, with the lantern, up and down the streets, knocking on doors, asking perfect strangers if they had seen you. O.K. That is certainly one way of doing it. This is not a complaint. But wouldn't it be better to openly acknowledge your utter reliance on work, on specific, carefully formulated directions, agreeing that, yes, a certain amount of anesthesia is derived from what other people would probably think of as some kind of a career? Excel if you want, but remember that there are gaps. You told me that you had thought, as a young girl, that masturbation was "only for men." Couldn't you be mistaken about other things, too?

The two sisters were looking at television in the bedroom, on the bed, amidst the coats and hats, umbrellas, airline bags. I gave them each a drink and we watched the game together, the *Osservatore Romano* team vs. the Diet of Worms, Worms leading by six points. I had never seen khaki-colored punch before. The hostess said there would be word games afterward, some of the people outside would be invited in, peasant food served in big wooden bowls—wine, chicken, olive oil, bread. Everything would improve, she said. I could still hear, outside, the drums; whistles had been added, there were both whistles and drums. I was surprised. The present era, with its emphasis on emotional cost control as well as its insistent, almost annoying lucidity, does not favor splinter groups, because they can't win. Small collective manifestations are O.K. insofar as they show "stretch marks"—traces of strain which tend to establish that public policy is not a smooth, seamless achievement, like an egg, but has rather been hammered out at some cost to the policymakers. Kong got to his feet. "Louise loves me," he said, pointing to a girl, "but I would rather sleep with Cynthia Garmonsway. It's just one of those things. Human experience is different, in some ways, from ape experience, but that doesn't mean that I don't like perfumed nights, too." I know what he means. The mind carries you with it, away from what you are supposed to do, toward things that cannot be explained rationally, toward difficulty, lack of clarity, late-afternoon light.

"Francesca. Do you want to go?"

"I want to stay."

Now the sisters have begun taking their interminable showers, both bathrooms are tied up, I must either pretend not to know them or accept the blame. In the larger rooms tender fawns and pinks have replaced the earlier drab, sad colors. I noticed that howls and rattles had been added to the whistles and drums. Is it some kind of a revolution? Maybe a revolution in taste, as when Mannerism was overthrown by the Baroque. Kong is being curried by Cynthia Garmonsway. She holds the steel curry comb in her right hand and pulls it gently through the dark thick fur. Cynthia formerly believed in the "enormous diversity of things"; now she believes in Kong. The man whose pronunciation I had corrected emerged from the kitchen. "Probably it is music," he said, nodding at the windows, "the new music, which we older men are too old to understand."

You, of course, would never say such a thing to me, but you have said worse things. You told me that Kafka was not a thinker, and that a "genetic" approach to his work would disclose that much of it was only a kind of very imaginative whining. That was during the period when you were going in for wrecking operations, feeling, I suppose, that the integrity of your own mental processes was best maintained by a series of strong, unforgiving attacks. You made quite an impression on everyone, in those days: your ruffled blouse, your long magenta skirt slit to the knee, the dagger thrust into your boot. "Is that a metaphor?" I asked, pointing to the dagger; you shook your head, smiled, said no. Now that you have had a change of heart, now that you have joined us in finding Kafka, and Kleist, too, the awesome figures that we have agreed that they are, the older faculty are more comfortable with you, are ready to promote you, marry you, even, if that is your wish. But you don't have to make up your mind tonight. Relax and enjoy the party, to the extent that it is possible to do so; it is not over yet. The game has ended, a news program has begun. "Emerald mines in the northwest have been nationalized." A number of young people standing in a meadow, holding hands, singing. Can the life of the time be caught in an advertisement? Is that how it is, really, in the meadows of the world?

And where are all the new people I have come here to meet? I have met only a lost child, dressed in rags, real rags, holding an iron hook attached to a fifty-foot rope. I said, "What is that for?" The child said nothing, placed the hook quietly on the floor at my feet, opened a bottle and swallowed twenty aspirin. Is six too young for a suicide attempt? We fed her milk, induced vomiting, the police arrived within minutes. When one has spoken a lot one has already used up all of the ideas one has. You must change the people you are speaking to so that you appear, to yourself, to be still alive. But the people here don't look new; they look like emerald-mine owners, in fact, or proprietors of some other sector of the economy that something bad has just happened to. I'm afraid that going up to them and saying "Travel light!," with a smile, will not really lift their spirits. Why am I called upon to make them happier, when it is so obviously beyond my competence? Francesca, you have selected the wrong partner, in me. You made the mistake a long time ago. I am not even sure that I like you now. But it is true that I cannot stop thinking about you, that every small daily problem—I will never be elected to the Academy, Richelieu is against me and d'Alembert is lukewarm—is examined in the light of your possible reaction, lack of reaction. At one moment you say that the Academy is a joke, at another that you are working industriously to sway Webster to my cause. Damned capricious! In the silence, an alphorn sounds. Then the noise again, drums, whistles, howls, rattles, alphorns. Attendants place heavy purple veils or shrouds over statuary, chairs, the buffet table, members of the orchestra. People are clustered in front of the bathrooms holding fine deep-piled towels, vying to dry the beautiful sisters. The towels move sensuously over the beautiful surfaces. I too could become excited over this prospect.

Dear Francesca, tell me, is this a successful party, in your view? Is this the best we can do? I know that you have always wanted to meet Kong; now that you have met him and he has said whatever he has said to you (I saw you smiling), can we go home? I mean you to your home, me to my home, all these others to their own homes, cells, cages? I am feeling a little ragged. What made us think that we would escape things like bankruptcy, alcoholism, being disappointed, having children? Say "No," refuse me once and for all, let me try something else. Of course we did everything right, insofar as we were able to imagine what "right" was. Is it really important to know that this movie is fine, and that one terrible, and to talk intelligently about the difference? Wonderful elegance! No good at all!

Engineer-Private Paul Klee Misplaces an Aircraft between Milbertshofen and Cambrai, March 1916

Paul Klee said:

"Now I have been transferred to the Air Corps. A kindly sergeant effected the transfer. He thought I would have a better future here, more chances for promotion. First I was assigned to aircraft repair, together with several other workers. We presented ourselves as not just painters but artist-painters. This caused some shaking of heads. We varnished wooden fuselages, correcting old numbers and adding new ones with the help of templates. Then I was pulled off the painting detail and assigned to transport. I escort aircraft that are being sent to various bases in Germany and also (I understand) in occupied territory. It is not a bad life. I spend my nights racketing across Bavaria (or some such) and my days in switching yards. There is always bread and wurst and beer in the station restaurants. When I reach a notable town I try to see the notable paintings there, if time allows. There are always unexpected delays, reroutings, backtrackings. Then the return to the base. I see Lily fairly often. We meet in hotel rooms and that is exciting. I have never yet lost an aircraft or failed to deliver one to its proper destination. The war seems interminable. Walden has sold six of my drawings.''

The Secret Police said:

''We have secrets. We have many secrets. We desire all secrets. We do not have your secrets and that is what we are after, your secrets. Our first secret is where we are. No one knows. Our second secret is how many of us there are. No one knows. Omnipresence is our goal. We do not even need real omnipresence, hand-in-hand as it were, goes omniscience. And with omniscience and omnipresence, hand-in-hand-in-hand as it were, goes omnipotence. We are a three-sided waltz. However our mood is melancholy. There is a secret sigh that we sigh, secretly. We yearn to be known, acknowledged, admired even. What is the good of omnipotence if nobody knows? However that is a secret, that sorrow. Now we are everywhere. One place we are is here watching Engineer-Private Klee, who is escorting three valuable aircraft, B.F.W. 3054/16–17–18, with spare parts, by rail from Milbertshofen to Cambrai. Do you wish to know what Engineer-Private Klee is doing at this very moment, in the baggage car? He is reading a book of Chinese short stories. He has removed his boots. His feet rest twenty-six centimeters from the baggage-car stove.''

Paul Klee said:

''These Chinese short stories are slight and lovely. I have no way of knowing if the translation is adequate or otherwise. Lily will meet me in our rented room on

Sunday, if I return in time. Our destination is Fighter Squadron Five. I have not had anything to eat since morning. The fine chunk of bacon given me along with my expense money when we left the base has been eaten. This morning a Red Cross lady with a squint gave me some very good coffee, however. Now we are entering Hohenbudberg."

The Secret Police said:

"Engineer-Private Klee has taken himself into the station restaurant. He is enjoying a hearty lunch. We shall join him there."

Paul Klee said:

"Now I emerge from the station restaurant and walk along the line of cars to the flatcar on which my aircraft (I think of them as *my* aircraft) are carried. To my surprise and dismay, I notice that one of them is missing. There had been three, tied down on the flatcar and covered with canvas. Now I see with my trained painter's eye that instead of three canvas-covered shapes on the flatcar there are only two. Where the third aircraft had been there is only a puddle of canvas and loose rope. I look around quickly to see if anyone else has marked the disappearance of the third aircraft."

The Secret Police said:

"We had marked it. Our trained policemen's eyes had marked the fact that where three aircraft had been before, tied down on the flatcar and covered with canvas, now there were only two. Unfortunately we had been in the station restaurant, lunching, at the moment of removal, therefore we could not attest as to where it had gone or who had removed it. There is something we do not know. This is irritating in the extreme. We closely observe Engineer-Private Klee to determine what action he will take in the emergency. We observe that he is withdrawing from his tunic a notebook and pencil. We observe that he begins, very properly in our opinion, to note down in his notebook all the particulars of the affair.''

Paul Klee said:

''The shape of the collapsed canvas, under which the aircraft had rested, together with the loose ropes—the canvas forming hills and valleys, seductive folds, the ropes the very essence of looseness, lapsing—it is irresistible. I sketch for ten or fifteen minutes, wondering the while if I might not be in trouble, because of the missing aircraft. When I arrive at Fighter Squadron Five with less than the number of aircraft listed on the manifest, might not some officious person become angry? Shout at me? I have finished sketching. Now I will ask various trainmen and station personnel if they have seen anyone carrying away the aircraft. If they answer in the negative, I will become extremely frustrated. I will begin to kick the flatcar.''

The Secret Police said:

''Frustrated, he begins to kick the flatcar.''

Paul Klee said:

''I am looking up in the sky, to see if my aircraft is there. There are in the sky aircraft of several types, but none of the type I am searching for.''

The Secret Police said:

''Engineer-Private Klee is searching the sky—an eminently sound procedure, in our opinion. We, the Secret Police, also sweep the Hohenbudberg sky, with our eyes. But find nothing. We are debating with ourselves as to whether we ought to enter the station restaurant and begin drafting our preliminary report, for forwarding to higher headquarters. The knotty point, in terms of the preliminary report, is that we do not have the answer to the question 'Where is the aircraft?' The damage potential to the theory of omniscience, as well as potential to our careers, dictates that this point be omitted from the preliminary report. But if this point is omitted, might not some officious person at the Central Bureau for Secrecy note the omission? Become angry? Shout at us? Omissiveness is not rewarded at the Central Bureau. We decide to observe further the actions of Engineer-Private Klee, for the time being.''

Paul Klee said:

"I who have never lost an aircraft have lost an aircraft. The aircraft is signed out to me. The cost of the aircraft, if it is not found, will be deducted from my pay, meager enough already. Even if Walden sells a hundred, a thousand drawings, I will not have enough money to pay for this cursed aircraft. Can I, in the time the train remains in the Hohenbudberg yards, construct a new aircraft or even the simulacrum of an aircraft, with no materials to work with or indeed any special knowledge of aircraft construction? The situation is ludicrous. I will therefore apply Reason. Reason dictates the solution. I will diddle the manifest. With my painter's skill which is after all not so different from a forger's, I will change the manifest to reflect conveyance of *two* aircraft, B.F.W. 3054/16 and 17, to Fighter Squadron Five. The extra canvas and ropes I will conceal in an empty boxcar—this one, which according to its stickers is headed for Essigny-le-Petit. Now I will walk around town and see if I can find a chocolate shop. I crave chocolate.''

The Secret Police said:

"Now we observe Engineer-Private Klee concealing the canvas and ropes which covered the former aircraft into an empty boxcar bound for Essigny-le-Petit. We have previously observed him diddling the manifest with his painter's skill which resembles not a little that of the forger. We applaud these actions of Engineer-

Private Klee. The contradiction confronting us in the matter of the preliminary report is thus resolved in highly satisfactory fashion. We are proud of Engineer-Private Klee and of the resolute and manly fashion in which he has dealt with the crisis. We predict he will go far. We would like to embrace him as a comrade and brother but unfortunately we are not embraceable. We are secret, we exist in the shadows, the pleasure of the comradely/brotherly embrace is one of the pleasures we are denied, in our dismal service."

Paul Klee said:

"We arrive at Cambrai. The planes are unloaded, six man for each plane. The work goes quickly. No one questions my altered manifest. The weather is clearing. After lunch I will leave to begin the return journey. My release slip and travel orders are ready, but the lieutenant must come and sign them. I wait contentedly in the warm orderly room. The drawing I did of the collapsed canvas and ropes is really very good. I eat a piece of chocolate. I am sorry about the lost aircraft but not overmuch. The war is temporary. But drawings and chocolate go on forever."

A Film

Things have never been better, except that the child, one of the stars of our film, has just been stolen by vandals, and this will slow down the progress of the film somewhat, if not bring it to a halt. But might not this incident, which is not without its own human drama, be made part of the story line? Julie places a hand on the child's head, in the vandal camp. "The fever has broken." The vandals give the child a wood doll to play with, until night comes. And suddenly I blunder into a landing party from our ships—forty lieutenants all in white, all holding their swords in front of their chins, in salute. The officer in charge slams his blade into its scabbard several times, in a gesture either decisive or indecisive. Yes, he will help us catch the vandals. No, he has no particular plan. Just general principles, he says. The Art of War itself.

The idea of the film is that it not be like other films.

SADNESS

* * *

I heard a noise outside. I looked out of the window. An old woman was bent over my garbage can, borrowing some of my garbage. They do that all over the city, old men and old women. They borrow your garbage and they never bring it back.

Thinking about the "Flying to America" sequence. This will be the film's climax. But am I capable of mounting such a spectacle? Fortunately I have Ezra to help.

"And is it not the case," said Ezra, when we first met, "that I have been associated with the production of nineteen major motion pictures of such savage originality, scalding *vérité,* and honey-warm sexual indecency that the very theaters chained their doors rather than permit exhibition of these major motion pictures on their ammonia-scented gum-daubed premises? And is it not the case," said Ezra, "that I myself with my two sinewy hands and strong-wrought God-gift brain have participated in the changing of seven high-class literary works of the first water and four of the second water and two of the third water into major muscatel? And is it not the living truth," said Ezra, "that I was the very man, I myself and none other without exception, who clung to the underside of the camera of the great Dreyer, clung with my two sinewy hands and noble thighs and cunning-muscled knees both dexter and sinister, during the cinematization of the master's *Gertrud,* clung there to slow the movement of said camera to that exquisite slowness which distinguishes this masterpiece from all other masterpieces of its water? And is it not chapter and verse," said Ezra, "that I was the comrade of all the comrades of the Dziga-Vertov group who was first in no-saying, fimest in no-saying, most final in no-saying, to all honey-sweet commercial seductions of whatever water and capitalist blandishments of whatever water and ideological incorrectitudes of whatever water whatsoever? And is it not as true as Saul become Paul," said Ezra, "that you require a man, a firm-limbed long-winded good true man, and that *I am the man* standing before you in his very blood and bones?"

"You are hired, Ezra," I said.

Whose child is it? We forgot to ask, when we sent out the casting call. Perhaps it belongs to itself. It has an air of self-possession quite remarkable in one so homely, and I notice that its paychecks are made out to it, rather than a nominee. Fortunately we have Julie to watch over it. The motor hotel in Tel Aviv is our temporary, not long-range, goal. New arrangements will probably not do the trick but we are making them anyhow: the ransom has been counted into pretty colored sacks, the film placed in round tin cans, the destroyed beams blocking the path are pushed aside . . .

Thinking of sequences for the film.
    A frenzy of desire?
    Sensible lovers taking precautions?
    Swimming with horses?

Today we filmed fear, a distressing emotion aroused by impending danger, real or imagined. In fear you know what you're afraid of, whereas in anxiety you do not. Correlation of children's fears with those of their parents is .667 according to Hagman. We filmed the startle pattern—shrinking, blinking, all that. Ezra refused to do "inhibition of the higher nervous centers." I don't blame him. However he was very good in demonstrating the sham rage reaction and also in "panting." Then we shot some stuff in which a primitive person (my bare arm standing in for the primitive person) kills an enemy by pointing a magic bone at him. "O.K., who's got the magic bone?" The magic bone was brought. I pointed the magic bone and the actor playing the enemy fell to the ground. I had carefully explained to the actor that the magic bone would not really kill him, probably.

Next, the thrill of fear along the buttocks. We used Julie's buttocks for this sequence. "Hope is the very sign of lack-of-happiness," said Julie, face down on the divan. "Fame is a palliative for doubt," I said. "Wealth-formation is a source of fear for both winners and losers," Ezra said. "Civilization aims at making all good things accessible even to cowards," said the actor who had played the enemy, quoting Nietzsche. Julie's buttocks thrilled.

We wrapped, then. I took the magic bone home with me. I don't believe in it, exactly, but you never know.

Have I ever been more alert, more confident? Following the dropped handkerchiefs to the vandal camp—there, a blue and green one, hanging on a shrub! The tall vandal chief wipes his hands on his sweatshirt. Vandals, he says, have been grossly misperceived. Their old practices, which earned them widespread condemnation, were a response to specific historical situations, and not a character trait, like being good or bad. Our negative has been scratched with a pointed instrument, all 150,000 feet of it. But the vandals say they were on the other side of town that night, planting trees. It is difficult to believe them. But gazing at the neat rows of saplings, carefully emplaced and surrounded by a vetchlike ground cover . . . A beautiful job! One does not know what to think.

We have got Frot Newling for the film; he will play the important role of George. Frot wanted many Gs in the beginning, but now that he understands the nature of the project he is working for scale, so that he can grow, as an actor and as a person. He is growing visibly, shot by shot. Soon he will be the biggest actor in the business. The other actors crowd about him, peering into his ankles . . . *Should* this film be made? That is one of the difficult questions one has to forget, when one is laughing in the face of unclear situations, or bad weather. What a beautiful girl Julie is! Her lustrous sexuality has the vandals agog. They follow her around trying to touch the tip of her glove, or the flounce of her gown. She shows her breasts to anyone who asks. "Amazing grace!" the vandals say.

Today we filmed the moon rocks. We set up in the Moon Rock Room, at the Smithsonian. There they were. The moon rocks. The moon rocks were the greatest thing we had ever seen in our entire lives! The moon rocks were red, green, blue, yellow, black, and white. They scintillated, sparkled, glinted, glittered, twinkled, and gleamed. They produced booms, thunderclaps, explosions, clashes, splashes, and roars. They sat on a pillow of the purest Velcro, and people who touched the pillow were able to throw away their crutches and jump in the air. Four cases of gout and eleven instances of hyperbolic paraboloidism were cured before our eyes. The air rained crutches. The moon rocks drew you toward them with a fatal irresistibility, but at the same time held you at a seemly distance with a decent reserve. Peering into the moon rocks, you could see the future and the past in color, and you could change them in any way you wished. The moon rocks gave off a slight hum, which cleaned your teeth, and a brilliant glow, which absolved you from sin. The moon rocks whistled *Finlandia,* by Jean Sibelius, while reciting *The Confessions of St. Augustine,* by I. F. Stone. The moon rocks were as good as a meaningful and emotionally rewarding seduction that you had not expected. The moon rocks were as good as listening to what the members of the Supreme Court say to each other, in the Supreme Court Locker Room. They were as good as a war. The moon rocks were better than a presentation copy of the *Random House Dictionary of the English Language* signed by Geoffrey Chaucer himself. They were better than a movie in which the President refuses to tell the people what to do to save themselves from the terrible thing that is about to happen, although he knows what ought to be done and has written a secret memorandum about it. The moon rocks were better than a good cup of coffee from an urn decorated with the change of Philomel, by the barbarous king. The moon rocks were better than a *¡huelga!* led by Mongo Santamaria, with additional dialogue by St. John of the Cross and special effects by Melmoth the Wanderer. The moon rocks surpassed our expectations. The dynamite out-of-sight very heavy and together moon rocks turned us on, to the highest degree. There was blood on our eyes, when we had finished filming them.

What if the film fails? And if it fails, will I know it?

A murdered doll floating face down in a bathtub—that will be the opening shot. A "cold" opening, but with faint intimations of the happiness of childhood and the pleasure we take in water. Then, the credits superimposed on a hanging side of beef. Samisen music, and a long speech from a vandal spokesman praising vandal culture and minimizing the sack of Rome in 455 A.D. Next, shots of a talk program in which all of the participants are whispering, including the host. Softness could certainly be considered a motif here. The child is well behaved through the long hours of shooting. The lieutenants march nicely, swinging their arms. The audience smiles. A vandal is standing near the window, and suddenly large cracks appear in the window. Pieces of glass fall to the floor. But I was watching him the whole time; he did nothing.

I wanted to film everything but there are things we are not getting. The wild ass is in danger in Ethiopia—we've got nothing on that. We've got nothing on intellectual elitism funded out of public money, an important subject. We've got nothing on ball lightning and nothing on the National Grid and not a foot on the core-mantle problem, the problem of a looped economy, or the interesting problem of the night brain.

I wanted to get it all but there's only so much time, so much energy. There's an increasing resistance to antibiotics worldwide and liquid metal fast-breeder reactors are subject to swelling and a large proportion of Quakers are color-blind but our film will have not a shred of material on any of these matters.

Is the film sufficiently sexual? I don't know.

I remember a brief exchange with Julie about revolutionary praxis.

"But I thought," I said, "that there had been a sexual

revolution and everybody could sleep with anybody who was a consenting adult.''

"In theory,'' Julie said. "In theory. But sleeping with someone also has a political dimension. One does not, for example, go to bed with running dogs of imperialism.''

I thought: But who will care for and solace the running dogs of imperialism? Who will bring them their dog food, who will tuck the covers tight as they dream their imperialistic dreams?

We press on. But where is Ezra? He was supposed to bring additional light, the light we need for "Flying to America.'' The vandals hit the trail, confused as to whether they should place themselves under our protection, or fight. The empty slivovitz bottles are buried, the ashes of the cooking fires scattered. At a signal from the leader the sleek, well-cared-for mobile homes swing onto the highway. The rehabilitation of the filmgoing public through "good design,'' through "softness,'' is our secret aim. The payment of rent for seats will be continued for a little while, but eventually abolished. Anyone will be able to walk into a film as into a shower. Bathing with the actors will become commonplace. Terror and terror are our two great principles, but we have other principles to fall back on, if these fail. "I can relate to that,'' Frot says. He does. We watch skeptically.

Who had murdered the doll? We pressed our inquiry, receiving every courtesy from the Tel Aviv police, who said they had never seen a case like it, either in their memories, or in dreams. A few wet towels were all the evidence that remained, except for, in the doll's hollow head, little pieces of paper on which were written

JULIE

JULIE

JULIE

JULIE

in an uncertain hand. And now the ground has opened up and swallowed our cutting room. One cannot really hold the vandals responsible. And yet . . .

Now we are shooting "Flying to America."

The 112 pilots check their watches.

Ezra nowhere to be seen. Will there be enough light?

If the pilots all turn on their machines at once . . .

Flying to America.

(But did I remember to—?)

"Where is the blimp?" Marcello shouts. "I can't find the—"

Ropes dangling from the sky.

I'm using forty-seven cameras, the outermost of which is posted in the Dover Marshes.

The Atlantic is calm in some parts, angry in others.

A blueprint four miles long is the flight plan.

Every detail coordinated with the air-sea rescue services of all nations.

Victory through Air Power! I seem to remember that slogan from somewhere.

Hovercraft flying to America. Flying boats flying to America. F-IIIs flying to America. The China Clipper!

Seaplanes, bombers, Flying Wings flying to America.

A shot of a pilot named Tom. He opens the cockpit door and speaks to the passengers. "America is only two thousand miles away now," he says. The passengers break out in smiles.

Balloons flying to America (they are painted in red-

and-white stripes). Spads and Fokkers flying to America. Self-improvement is a large theme in flying to America. "Nowhere is self-realization more a possibility than in America," a man says.

Julie watching the clouds of craft in the air . . .

Gliders gliding to America. One man has constructed a huge paper aircraft, seventy-two feet in length. It is doing better than we had any right to expect. But then great expectations are an essential part of flying to America.

Rich people are flying to America, and poor people, and people of moderate means. This aircraft is powered by twelve rubber bands, each rubber band thicker than a man's leg—can it possibly survive the turbulence over Greenland?

Long thoughts are extended to enwrap the future American experience of the people who are flying to America.

And here is Ezra! and Ezra is carrying the light we need for this part of the picture—a great bowl of light lent to us by the U.S. Navy. Now our film will be successful, or at least completed, and the aircraft illuminated, and the child will be rescued, and Julie will marry well, and the light from the light will fall into the eyes of the vandals, fixing them in place. Truth! That is another thing they said our film wouldn't contain. I had simply forgotten about it, in contemplating the series of triumphs that is my private life.

The Sandman

Dear Dr. Hodder, I realize that it is probably wrong to write a letter to one's girl friend's shrink but there are several things going on here that I think ought to be pointed out to you. I thought of making a personal visit but the situation then, as I'm sure you understand, would be completely untenable—I would be *visiting a psychiatrist.* I also understand that in writing to you I am in some sense interfering with the process but you don't have to discuss with Susan what I have said. Please consider this an "eyes only" letter. Please think of it as personal and confidential.

You must be aware, first, that because Susan is my girl friend pretty much everything she discusses with you she also discusses with me. She tells me what she said and what you said. We have been seeing each other for about six months now and I am pretty familiar with her story, or stories. Similarly, with your responses, or at least the general pattern. I know, for example, that my habit of referring to you as "the sandman" annoys you but let me assure you that I mean nothing unpleasant by it. It is simply a nickname. The reference is to the old rhyme: "Sea-sand does the sandman bring/Sleep to end the day/He dusts the children's eyes with sand/ And steals their dreams away." (This is a variant; there are other versions, but this is the one I prefer.) I also understand that you are a little bit shaky because the prestige of analysis is now, as I'm sure you know far better than I, at a nadir. This must tend to make you nervous and who can blame you? One always tends to get a little bit shook when one's methodology is in question. Of course! (By the bye, let me say that I am very pleased that you are one of the ones that talk, instead of just sitting there. I think that's a good thing, an excellent thing, I congratulate you.)

To the point. I fully understand that Susan's wish to terminate with you and buy a piano instead has disturbed you. You have every right to be disturbed and to say that she is not electing the proper course, that what she says conceals something else, that she is evading reality, etc., etc. Go ahead. But there is one possibility here that you might be, just might be, missing. Which is that she means it.

Susan says: "I want to buy a piano."

You think: She wishes to terminate the analysis and escape into the piano.

Or: Yes, it is true that her father wanted her to be a concert pianist and that she studied for twelve years with Goetzmann. But she does not really want to reopen that can of maggots. She wants me to disapprove.

Or: Having failed to achieve a career as a concert pianist, she wishes to fail again. She is now too old to achieve the original objective. The spontaneous organization of defeat!

Or: She is flirting again.

Or:

Or:

Or:

Or:

The one thing you cannot consider, by the nature of your training and of the discipline itself, is that she really might want to terminate the analysis and buy a piano. That the piano might be more necessary and valuable to her than the analysis.[1]

What we really have to consider here is the locus of hope. Does hope reside in the analysis or rather in the piano? As a shrink rather than a piano salesman you would naturally tend to opt for the analysis. But there are differences. The piano salesman can stand behind his product; you, unfortunately, cannot. A Steinway is a known quantity, whereas an analysis can succeed or fail. I don't reproach you for this, I simply note it. (An interesting question: Why do laymen feel such a desire to, in plain language, fuck over shrinks? As I am doing here, in a sense? I don't mean hostility in the psychoanalytic encounter, I mean in general. This is an interesting phenomenon and should be investigated by somebody.)

It might be useful if I gave you a little taste of my own experience of analysis. I only went five or six times. Dr. Behring was a tall thin man who never said anything much. If you could get a "What comes to mind?" out of

---

[1]For an admirable discussion of this sort of communication failure and many other matters of interest see Percy, "Toward a Triadic Theory of Meaning," *Psychiatry,* Vol. 35 (February 1972), pp. 6–14 *et seq.*

him you were doing splendidly. There was a little incident that is, perhaps, illustrative. I went for my hour one day and told him about something I was worried about. (I was then working for a newspaper down in Texas.) There was a story that four black teenagers had come across a little white boy, about ten, in a vacant lot, sodomized him repeatedly and then put him inside a refrigerator and closed the door (this was before they had that requirement that abandoned refrigerators had to have their doors removed) and he suffocated. I don't know to this day what actually happened, but the cops had picked up *some* black kids and were reportedly beating the shit out of them in an effort to make them confess. I was not on the police run at that time but one of the police reporters told me about it and I told Dr. Behring. A good liberal, he grew white with anger and said what was I doing about it? It was the first time he had talked. So I was shaken—it hadn't occurred to me that I was required to do something about it, he was right—and after I left I called my then sister-in-law, who was at that time secretary to a City Councilman. As you can imagine, such a position is a very powerful one— the councilmen are mostly off making business deals and the executive secretaries run the office—and she got on to the chief of police with an inquiry as to what was going on and if there was any police brutality involved and if so, how much. The case was a very sensational one, you see; *Ebony* had a writer down there trying to cover it but he couldn't get in to see the boys and the cops had roughed him up some, they couldn't understand at that time that there could be such a thing as a black reporter. They understood that they had to be a little careful with the white reporters, but a black reporter was beyond them. But my sister-in-law threw her weight (her Councilman's weight) around a bit and suggested to the chief that if there was a serious amount of brutality going on the cops had better stop it, because there was too much outside interest in the case and it would be extremely bad PR if the brutality stuff got out. I also called a guy I knew pretty high up in the sheriff's department and suggested that *he* suggest to his colleagues that they cool it. I hinted at unspeakable political urgencies and he picked it up. The sheriff's department was separate from the police department but they both operated out of the Courthouse Building and they interacted quite a bit, in the normal course. So the long and short of it was that the cops decided to show the four black kids at a press conference to demonstrate that they weren't really beat all to rags, and that took place at four in the afternoon. I went and the kids looked O.K., except for one whose teeth were out and who the cops said had fallen down the stairs. Well, we all know the falling-down-the-stairs story but the point was the *degree* of mishandling and it was clear that the kids had not been half-killed by the cops, as the rumor stated. They were walking and talking naturally, although scared to death, as who would not be? There weren't any TV pictures because the newspaper people always pulled out the plugs of the TV people, at important moments, in those days—it was a standard thing. Now while I admit it sounds callous to be talking about the degree of brutality being minimal, let me tell you that it was no small matter, in that time and place, to force the cops to show the kids to the press at all. It was an achievement, of sorts. So about eight o'clock I called Dr. Behring at home, I hope interrupting his supper, and told him that the kids were O.K., relatively, and he said that was fine, he was glad to hear it. They were later no-billed and I stopped seeing him. That was my experience of analysis and that it may have left me a little sour, I freely grant. Allow for this bias.

To continue. I take exception to your remark that Susan's "openness" is a form of voyeurism. This remark interested me for a while, until I thought about it. Voyeurism I take to be an eroticized expression of curiosity whose chief phenomenological characteristic is the distance maintained between the voyeur and the object. The tension between the desire to draw near the object and the necessity to maintain the distance becomes a libidinous energy nondischarge, which is what the voyeur seeks.[2] The tension. But your remark indicates, in my opinion, a radical misreading of the problem. Susan's "openness"—a willingness of the heart, if you will allow such a term—is not at all comparable to the activities of the voyeur. Susan draws near. Distance is not her thing—not by a long chalk. Frequently, as you know, she gets burned, but she always tries again. What is operating here, I suggest, is an attempt on your part to "stabilize" Susan's behavior in reference to a state-of-affairs that you feel should obtain. Susan gets married and lives happily ever after. Or: There is within Susan a certain amount of creativity which should be liberated and actualized. Susan becomes an artist and lives happily ever after.

But your norms are, I suggest, skewing your view of the problem, and very badly.

Let us take the first case. You reason: If Susan is happy or at least functioning in the present state of affairs (that is, moving from man to man as a silver dollar moves from hand to hand), then why is she seeing a shrink? Something is wrong. New behavior is in-

---

[2]See, for example, Straus, "Shame As a Historiological Problem," in *Phenomenological Psychology* (New York: Basic Books, 1966), p. 219.

dicated. Susan is to get married and live happily ever after. May I offer another view? That is, that "seeing a shrink" might be precisely a maneuver in a situation in which Susan *does not want* to get married and live happily ever after? That getting married and living happily ever after might be, for Susan, the worst of fates, and that in order to validate her nonacceptance of this norm she defines herself to herself as shrink-needing? That you are actually certifying the behavior which you seek to change? (When she says to you that she's not shrinkable, you should listen.)

Perhaps, Dr. Hodder, my logic is feeble, perhaps my intuitions are frail. It is, God knows, a complex and difficult question. Your perception that Susan is an artist of some kind *in potentia* is, I think, an acute one. But the proposition "Susan becomes an artist and lives happily ever after" is ridiculous. (I realize that I am couching the proposition in such terms—"happily ever after"—that it is ridiculous on the face of it, but there is ridiculousness piled upon ridiculousness.) Let me point out, if it has escaped your notice, that what an artist does, is fail. Any reading of the literature[3] (I mean the theory of artistic creation), however summary, will persuade you instantly that the paradigmatic artistic experience is that of failure. The actualization fails to meet, equal, the intuition. There is something "out there" which cannot be brought "here." This is standard. I don't mean bad artists, I mean good artists. There is no such thing as a "successful artist" (except, of course, in worldly terms). The proposition should read, "Susan becomes an artist and lives unhappily ever after." This is the case. Don't be deceived.

---

[3] Expecially, perhaps, Ehrenzweig, *The Hidden Order of Art* (University of California Press, 1966), pp. 234–9.

What I am saying is, that the therapy of choice is not clear. I deeply sympathize. You have a dilemma.

I ask you to note, by the way, that Susan's is not a seeking after instant gratification as dealt out by so-called encounter or sensitivity groups, nude marathons, or dope. None of this is what is going down. "Joy" is not Susan's bag. I praise her for seeking out you rather than getting involved with any of this other idiocy. Her forte, I would suggest, is mind, and if there are games being played they are being conducted with taste, decorum, and some amount of intellectual rigor. Not-bad games. When I take Susan out to dinner she does not order chocolate-covered ants, even if they are on the menu. (Have you, by the way, tried Alfredo's, at the corner of Bank and Hudson streets? It's wonderful.) (Parenthetically, the problem of analysts sleeping with their patients is well known and I understand that Susan has been routinely seducing you—a reflex, she can't help it—throughout the analysis. I understand that there is a new splinter group of therapists, behaviorists of some kind, who take this to be some kind of ethic? Is this true? Does this mean that they do it only when they want to, or whether they want to or not? At a dinner party the other evening a lady analyst was saying that three cases of this kind had recently come to her attention and she seemed to think that this was rather a lot. The problem of maintaining mentorship is, as we know, not easy. I think you have done very well in this regard, and God knows it must have been difficult, given those skirts Susan wears that unbutton up to the crotch and which she routinely leaves unbuttoned to the third button.)

Am I wandering too much for you? Bear with me. The world is waiting for the sunrise.

We are left, I submit, with the problem of her

depressions. They are, I agree, terrible. Your idea that I am not "supportive" enough is, I think, wrong. I have found, as a practical matter, that the best thing to do is to just do ordinary things, read the newspaper for example, or watch basketball, or wash the dishes. That seems to allow her to come out of it better than any amount of so-called "support." (About the *chasmus hystericus* or hysterical yawning I don't worry any more. It is masking behavior, of course, but after all, you must allow us our tics. The world is waiting for the sunrise.) What do you do with a patient who finds the world unsatisfactory? The world *is* unsatisfactory; only a fool would deny it. I know that your own ongoing psychic structuralization is still going on—you are thirty-seven and I am forty-one—but you must be old enough by now to realize that shit is shit. Susan's perception that America has somehow got hold of the greed ethic and that the greed ethic has turned America into a tidy little hell is not, I think, wrong. What do you do with such a perception? Apply Band-Aids, I suppose. About her depressions, I wouldn't do anything. I'd leave them alone. Put on a record.[4]

Let me tell you a story.

One night we were at her place, about three a.m., and this man called, another lover, quite a well-known musician who is very good, very fast—a good man. He asked Susan "Is he there?," meaning me, and she said "Yes," and he said "What are you doing?," and she said, "What do you think?," and he said, "When will you be finished?," and she said, "Never." Are you, Doctor dear, in a position to appreciate the beauty of this reply, in this context?

---

[4]For example, Harrison, "Wah Wah," Apple Records, STCH 639, Side One, Track 3.

What I am saying is that Susan is wonderful. *As is.* There are not so many things around to which that word can be accurately applied. Therefore I must view your efforts to improve her with, let us say, a certain amount of ambivalence. If this makes me a negative factor in the analysis, so be it. I will be a negative factor until the cows come home, and cheerfully. I can't help it, Doctor, I am voting for the piano.

With best wishes,

Departures

1.

I cashed a fifty-dollar Defense Bond given me by my older brother and ran away from home. We stood by the roadside, myself and a colleague who was also running away from home, holding out our hands. This was in Texas, during the War. An old Hudson stopped. Inside were a black man, who was driving, a white man, who was sitting in the death seat, and a small Oriental-looking woman, who was sitting in back. "Where you goin'?" the black man asked. "Mexico City," we said. We were wearing jeans and T-shirts. "O.K.," the black man said, "get in." The white man in the front seat began telling us about himself. He was a songwriter, he said. He had written "Drinking Lemonade in Kentucky in the Morning." Had we ever heard that one? We said no, indicating that the fault was ours—pure ignorance. He had lived in Hawaii for a long time, he said. His wife back there was Hawaiian. The black man was a professional jazz drummer. They were headed for Mexico City, by a striking coincidence. They all lived together in Mexico City, D.F., and had a business there.

We crossed the border at Laredo. My friend Herman and I had changed all the money we had into one-peso notes with a fifty-peso note on the outside of the wad. We showed the wad to the border officials demonstrating that we would not become a burden upon the State. We had learned this device from the movies.

After the second border checkpoint had been passed, the car stopped at a house and everybody got out to change the tires. The drummer and the songwriter pried the tires off the rims. Herman and I helped. Copper wire, hundreds of feet of it, was wound round each of the rims. Our friends were smuggling copper wire, a scarce item during the War. The benefits of leaving home were borne in on us. We had never met any absolutely genuine smugglers before.

When we got to Mexico City, the songwriter and the drummer gave us jobs in their business which was importing American jukeboxes and converting them into Mexican jukeboxes. Our job was to file the coin slots of the jukeboxes into larger slots so that they would accept Mexican coins, which tend to be large. We stayed there a week. Then we went home.

2.

ARMY PLANS TO FREEZE
3 MILLION BIRDS TO DEATH

MILAN, Tenn., Feb. 14 (AP)—The Army is planning to freeze to death three million or so blackbirds that took up residence two years ago at the Milan Arsenal.

Paul Lefebvre of the U.S. Department of the Interior, which is also working on the plan, said yesterday that the birds would be sprayed with two chemicals, resulting in a rapid loss of body heat. This will be done on a night with sub-freezing temperatures, he said.

3.

There is an elementary school, P.S. 421, across the street from my building. Now the Board of Education is busing children from the bad areas of the city to P.S. 421 (our area is thought to be a good area) and busing children from P.S. 421 to schools in the bad areas, in order to achieve racial balance in the schools. The parents of the P.S. 421 children do not like this very much, but they are all good citizens and feel it must be done. The parents of the children in the bad areas may not like it much, either, having their children so far from home, but they too probably feel that the process makes somehow for a better education. Every morning the green buses arrive in front of the school, some bringing black and Puerto Rican children to P.S. 421 and others taking the local, mostly white, children away. Presiding over all this is the loadmaster.

The loadmaster is a heavy, middle-aged white woman, not fat but heavy, who wears a blue cloth coat and a scarf around her head and carries a clipboard. She gets the children into and out of the buses, briskly, briskly, shouting, "Let's go, let's go, LET'S GO!" She has a voice that is louder than the voices of forty children. She gets a bus filled up, gives her clipboard a fast once-over, and sends the driver on his way: "O.K., José." The bus has been parked in the middle of the street, and there is a long line of hungup cars behind it, unable to pass, their drivers blowing their horns impatiently. When the drivers of these cars honk their horns too vigorously, the loadmaster steps away from the bus and yells at them in a voice louder than fourteen stacked-up drivers blowing their horns all at once: "KEEP YOUR PANTS ON!" Then to the bus driver: "O.K., José." As the bus starts off, she stands back giving it an authoritative smack on its rump (much like a coach sending a fresh player into the game) as it passes. Then she waves the stacked-up drivers on their way, one authoritative wave for each driver. She is making authoritative motions long after there is any necessity for it.

4.

DUNKIRK

5.

My grandfather once fell in love with a dryad—a wood nymph who lives in trees and to whom trees are sacred and who dances around trees clad in fine leaf-green tutu and who carries a great silver-shining axe to whack anybody who does any kind of thing inimical to the well-being and mental health of trees. My grandfather was at that time in the lumber business.

It was during the Great War. He'd got an order for a million board feet of one-by-ten of the very poorest quality, to make barracks out of for the soldiers. The specifications called for the dark red sap to be running off it in buckets and for the warp on it to be like the tops of waves in a distressed sea and for the knotholes in it to be the size of an intelligent man's head for the cold wind to whistle through and toughen up the (as they were then called) doughboys.

My grandfather headed for East Texas. He had the timber rights to ten thousand acres then, Southern yellow pine of the loblolly family. It was third-growth scrub and slash and shoddy—just the thing for soldiers. Couldn't be beat. So he and his men set up operations and first crack out of the box they were surrounded by threescore of lovely dryads and hamadryads all clad in fine leaf-green tutus and waving great silver-shining axes.

"Well now," my grandfather said to the head dryad, "wait a while, wait a while, somebody could get hurt."

"That is for sure," says the girl, and she shifts her axe from her left hand to her right hand.

"I thought you dryads were indigenous to oak," says my grandfather, "this here is pine."

"Some like the ancient tall-standing many-branched oak," says the girl, "and some the white-slim birch, and some take what they can get, and you will look mighty funny without any legs on you."

"Can we negotiate," says my grandfather, "it's for the War, and you are the loveliest thing I ever did see, and what is your name?"

"Megwind," says the girl, "and also Sophie. I am Sophie in the night and Megwind in the day and I make fine whistling axe-music night or day and without legs for walking your life's journey will be a pitiable one."

"Well Sophie," says my grandfather, "let us sit down under this tree here and open a bottle of this fine rotgut here and talk the thing over like reasonable human beings."

"Do not use my night-name in the light of day," says the girl, "and I am not a human being and there is nothing to talk over and what type of rotgut is it that you have there?"

"It is Teamster's Early Grave," says my grandfather, "and you'll cover many a mile before you find the beat of it."

"I will have one cupful," says the girl, "and my sisters will have each one cupful, and then we will dance around this tree while you still have legs for dancing and then you will go away and your men also."

"Drink up," says my grandfather, "and know that of all the women I have interfered with in my time you are the absolute top woman."

"I am not a woman," says Megwind, "I am a spirit, although the form of the thing is misleading I will admit."

"Wait a while," says my grandfather, "you mean that no type of mutual interference between us of a physical nature is possible."

"That is a thing I could do," says the girl, "if I chose."

"Do you choose?" asks my grandfather, "and have another wallop."

"That is a thing I will do," says the girl, and she had another wallop.

"And a kiss," says my grandfather, "would that be possible do you think?"

"That is a thing I could do," says the dryad, "you are not the least prepossessing of men and men have been scarce in these parts in these years, the trees being as you see mostly scrub, slash and shoddy."

"Megwind," says my grandfather, "you are beautiful."

"You are taken with my form which I admit is beautiful," says the girl, "but know that this form you see is not necessary but contingent, sometimes I am a fine brown-speckled egg and sometimes I am an escape of steam from a hole in the ground and sometimes I am an armadillo.''

"That is amazing," says my grandfather, "a shape-shifter are you."

"That is a thing I can do," says Megwind, "if I choose.''

"Tell me," says my grandfather, "could you change yourself into one million board feet of one-by-ten of the very poorest quality neatly stacked in railroad cars on a siding outside of Fort Riley, Kansas?''

"That is a thing I could do," says the girl, "but I do not see the beauty of it.''

"The beauty of it," says my grandfather, "is two cents a board foot.''

"What is the *quid pro quo?*" asks the girl.

"You mean spirits engage in haggle?" asks my grandfather.

"Nothing from nothing, nothing for nothing, that is a law of life," says the girl.

"The *quid pro quo*," says my grandfather, "is that me and my men will leave this here scrub, slash and shoddy standing. All you have to do is to be made into barracks for the soldiers and after the War you will be torn down and can fly away home.''

"Agreed," says the dryad, "but what about this interference of a physical nature you mentioned earlier? for the sun is falling down and soon I will be Sophie and human men have been scarce in these parts for ever so damn long.''

"Sophie," says my grandfather, "you are as lovely as light and let me just fetch another bottle from the truck and I will be at your service.''

This is not really how it went. I am fantasizing. Actually, he just plain cut down the trees.

6.

I was on an operating table. My feet were in sterile bags. My hands and arms were wrapped in sterile towels. A sterile bib covered my beard. A giant six-eyed light was shining in my eyes. I closed my eyes. There was a doctor on the right side of my head and a doctor on the left side of my head. The doctor on the right was my doctor. The doctor on the left was studying the art. He was Chinese, the doctor on the left. My doctor spoke to the nurse who was handing him tools. *"Rebecca! You're not supposed to be holding conversations with the circulating nurse, Rebecca. You're suppose to be watching me, Rebecca!"* We had all gathered here in this room to cut out part of my upper lip into which a basal-cell malignancy had crept.

In my mind, the basal-cell malignancy resembled a tiny truffle.

"Most often occurs in sailors and farmers," the doctor had told me. "The sun." But I, I sit under General Electric light, mostly. "We figure you can lose up to a third of it, the lip, without a bad result," the doctor had told me. "There's a lot of stretch." He had demonstrated upon his own upper lip, stretching it with his two forefingers. The doctor a large handsome man with silver spectacles. In my hospital room, I listened to my Toshiba transistor, Randy Newman singing "Let's Burn Down the Cornfield." I was waiting for the morning, for the operation. A friendly Franciscan entered in his brown robes. "Why is it that in the space under 'Religion' on your form you entered 'None'?" he asked in a friendly way. I considered the question. I rehearsed for him my religious history. We discussed the distinguishing characteristics of the various religious orders—the Basilians, the Capuchins. Recent outbreaks of Enthusiasm among the Dutch Catholics were touched upon. "Rebecca!" the doctor said, in the operating room. *"Watch me, Rebecca!"*

I had been given a morphine shot along with various locals in the lip. I was feeling very good! The Franciscan had lived in the Far East for a long time. I too had been in the Far East. The Army band had played, as we climbed the ramp into the hold of the troopship, "Bye Bye Baby, Remember You're My Baby." "We want a good result," my original doctor had said, "because of the prominence of the—" He pointed to my upper lip. "So I'm sending you to a good man." This seemed sensible. I opened my eyes. The bright light. "Give me a No. 10 blade," the doctor said. "Give me a No. 15 blade." Something was certainly going on there, above my teeth. "Gently, gently," my doctor said to his colleague. The next morning a tiny Thai nurse came in bringing me orange juice, orange Jell-O, and an orange broth. "Is there any pain?" she asked.

My truffle was taken to the pathologist for examination. I felt the morphine making me happy. I thought: What a beautiful hospital.

A handsome nurse from Jamaica came in. "Now you put this on," she said, handing me a wrinkled white garment without much back to it. "No socks. No shorts."

No shorts!

I climbed onto a large moving bed and was wheeled to the operating table, where the doctors were preparing themselves for the improvement of my face. My doctor invited the Chinese doctor to join him in a scrub. I was eating my orange Jell-O, my orange broth. My wife called and said that she had eaten a superb beef

Wellington for dinner, along with a good bottle. Every time I smiled the stitches jerked tight.

I was standing outside the cashier's window. I had my pants on and was feeling very dancy. "Udbye!" I said. "Hank you!"

7.

I went to a party. I saw a lady I knew. "Hello!" I said. "Are you pregnant?" She was wearing what appeared to be maternity clothes.

"No," she said, "I am not."

"Cab!"

8.

But where are you today?

Probably out with your husband for a walk. He has written another beautiful poem, and needs the refreshment of the air. I admire him. Everything he does is successful. He is wanted for lectures in East St. Louis, at immense fees. I admire him, but my admiration for you is . . . Do you think he has noticed? What foolishness! It is as obvious as a bumper sticker, as obvious as an abdication.

Your Royal Canadian Mounted Police hat set squarely across the wide white brow . . .

Your white legs touching each other, under the banquet table . . .

Probably you are walking with your husband in SoHo, seeing what the new artists are refusing to do there, in their quest for a scratch to start from.

The artists regard your brown campaign hat, your white legs. "Holy God!" they say, and return to their lofts.

I have spent many message units seeking your voice, but I always get Frederick instead.

"Well, Frederick," I ask cordially, "what amazing triumphs have you accomplished today?"

He has been offered a sinecure at Stanford and a cenotaph at C.C.N.Y. Bidding for world rights to his breath has begun at $500,000.

But I am wondering—

When you placed your hand on my napkin, at the banquet, did that mean anything?

When you smashed in the top of my soft-boiled egg for me, at the banquet, did that indicate that I might continue to hope?

I will name certain children after you. (People often ask my advice about naming things.) I will be suspicious, so many small Philippas popping up in our city, but the pattern will only become visible with the passage of time, and in the interval, what satisfaction!

I cannot imagine the future. You have not made your intentions clear, if indeed you have any. What is the point of all this misery? I am a voter! I am a veteran! I am forty! My life is insured! Now you are climbing aboard a great ship, and the hawsers are being loosed, and the flowers in the cabins arranged, and the dinner gong sounded. I am sure you will eat well aboard that ship, but you don't understand—it is sailing away from me!

Subpoena

And now in the mail a small white Subpoena from the Bureau of Compliance, Citizen Bergman there, he wants me to comply. *We command you that, all business and excuses being laid aside, you and each of you appear and attend* . . . The "We command you" in boldface, and a shiny red seal in the lower left corner. To get my attention.

I thought I had complied. I comply every year, sometimes oftener than necessary. Look at the record. Spotless list of compliances dating back to '48, when I was a pup. What can he mean, this Bergman, finding a freckle on my clean sheet?

I appeared and attended. Attempted to be reasonable. "Look here Bergman what is this business." Read him an essay I'd written about how the State should not muck about in the affairs of its vassals overmuch. Citizen Bergman unamused.

"It appears that you are the owner or proprietor perhaps of a monster going under the name of Charles Evans Hughes?"

"Yes but what has that to do with—"

"Said monster inhabiting quarters at 12 Tryst Lane?"

"That is correct."

"This monster being of humanoid appearance and characteristics, including ability to locomote, production of speech of a kind, ingestion of viands, and traffic with other beings?"

"Well, 'traffic' is hardly the word. Simple commands he can cope with. Nothing fancy. Sit. Eat. Speak. Roll over. Beg. That sort of thing."

"This monster being employed by you in the capacity, friend?"

"Well, employed is not quite right."

"He is remunerated is he not?"

"The odd bit of pocket money."

"On a regular basis."

"See here Bergman it's an allowance. For little things he needs. Cigarettes and handkerchiefs and the like. Nose drops."

"He is nevertheless in receipt of sums of money from you on a regular basis?"

"He is forty-four percent metal, Officer."

"The metal content of said monster does not interest the Bureau. What we are interested in is compliance."

"Wherein have I failed to comply?"

"You have not submitted Form 244 which governs paid companionship, including liaisons with prostitutes and pushing of wheelchairs by hired orderlies not provided by the Bureau of Perpetual Help. You have also failed to remit the Paid Companionship Tax which amounts to one hundred twenty-two percent of all moneys changing hands in any direction."

"One hundred twenty-two percent!"

"That is the figure. There is also a penalty for

noncompliance. The penalty is two hundred twelve percent of one hundred twenty-two percent of five dollars a week figured over five years, which I believe is the period at issue."

"What about depreciation?"

"Depreciation is not figurable in the case of monsters."

I went home feeling less than sunny.

He had a knowing look that I'd painted myself. One corner of the mouth curled upward and the other downward, when he smiled. There was no grave-robbing or anything of that sort. Plastic and metal did very nicely. You can get the most amazing things in drugstores. Fingernails and eyelashes and such. The actual construction was a matter of weeks. I considered sending the plans to *Popular Mechanics*. So that everyone could have one.

He was calm—calm as a hat. Whereas I was nervous as a strobe light, had the shakes, Valium in the morning and whiskey beginning at two o'clock in the afternoon.

Everything was all right with him.

"Crushed in an elevator at the welfare hotel!" someone would say.

"It's a very serious problem," Charles would answer.

When I opened the door, he was sitting in the rocking chair reading *Life*.

"Charles," I said, "they've found out."

"Seventy-seven percent of American high-school students declare that religion is important to them, according to a recent Louis Harris poll," Charles said, rocking gently.

"Charles," I said, "they want money. The Paid

Companionship Tax. It's two hundred twelve percent of one hundred twenty-two percent of five dollars a week figured over five years, plus of course the basic one hundred twenty-two percent."

"That's a lot of money," Charles said, smiling. "A pretty penny."

"I can't pay," I said. "It's too much."

"Well," he said, both smiling and rocking, "fine. What are you going to do?"

"Disassemble," I said.

"Interesting," he said, hitching his chair closer to mine, to demonstrate interest. "Where will you begin?"

"With the head, I suppose."

"Wonderful," Charles said. "You'll need the screwdriver, the pliers, and the Skil-saw. I'll fetch them."

He got up to go to the basement. A thought struck him. "Who will take out the garbage?" he asked.

"Me. I'll take it out myself."

He smiled. One corner of his mouth turned upward and the other downward. "Well," he said, "right on."

I called him my friend and thought of him as my friend. In fact I kept him to instruct me in complacency. He sat there, the perfect noncombatant. He ate and drank and slept and awoke and did not change the world. Looking at him I said to myself, "See, it is possible to live in the world and not change the world." He read the newspapers and watched television and heard in the night screams under windows thank God not ours but down the block a bit, and did nothing. Without Charles, without his example, his exemplary quietude, I run the risk of acting, the risk of risk. I must participate, I must leave the house and walk about.

The Catechist

In the evenings, usually, the catechist approaches. "Where have you been?" he asks.

"In the park," I say.

"Was she there?" he asks.

"No," I say.

The catechist is holding a book. He reads aloud: "*The chief reason for Christ's coming was to manifest and teach God's love for us. Here the catechist should find the focal point of his instruction.*" On the word "manifest" the catechist places the tip of his right forefinger upon the tip of his left thumb, and on the word "teach" the catechist places the tip of his right forefinger upon the tip of his left forefinger.

Then he says: "And the others?"

I say: "Abusing the mothers."

"The guards?"

"Yes. As usual."

The catechist reaches into his pocket and produces a newspaper clipping. "Have you heard the news?" he asks.

"No," I say.

He reads aloud: *"Vegetable Oil Allowed in Three Catholic Rites."*

He pauses. He looks at me. I say nothing. He reads aloud: *"Rome, March 2nd. Reuters."* He looks at me. I say nothing. *"Reuters,"* he repeats. *"Roman Catholic sacramental anointings may in the future be performed with any vegetable oil, according to a new Vatican ruling that lifts the Church's age-old—"* He pauses. *"Age-old,"* he emphasizes.

I think: Perhaps she is at ease. Looking at her lake.

The catechist reads: *". . . that lifts the Church's age-old insistence on the use of olive oil. New paragraph. Under Catholic ritual, holy oil previously blessed by a bishop is used symbolically in the sacraments of confirmation, baptism, and the anointing of the sick, formerly extreme unction. New paragraph. Other vegetable oils are cheaper and considerably easier to obtain than olive oil in many parts of the world, Vatican observers noted."* The catechist pauses. "You're a priest. I'm a priest," he says. "Now I ask you."

I think: Perhaps she is distressed and looking at the lake does nothing to mitigate the distress.

He says: "Consider that you are dying. The sickroom. The bed. The plucked-at sheets. The distraught loved ones. The priest approaches. Bearing the only viaticum, the sacred oils. The administration of the Host. The last anointing. And what is it you're given? You, the dying man? Peanut oil."

I think: Peanut oil.

The catechist replaces the clipping in his pocket. He

will read it to me again tomorrow. Then he says: "When you saw the guards abusing the mothers, you—"

I say: "Wrote another letter."

"And you mailed the letter?"

"As before."

"The same mailbox?"

"Yes."

"You remembered to put a stamp—"

"An eight-cent Eisenhower."

I think: When I was young they asked other questions.

He says: "Tell me about her."

I say: "She has dark hair."

"Her husband—"

"I don't wish to discuss her husband."

The catechist reads from his book. *"The candidate should be questioned as to his motives for becoming a Christian."*

I think: My motives?

He says: "Tell me about yourself."

I say: "I'm forty. I have bad eyes. An enlarged liver."

"That's the alcohol," he says.

"Yes," I say.

"You're very much like your father, there."

"A shade more avid."

We have this conversation every day. No detail changes. He says: "But a man in your profession—"

I say: "But I don't want to discuss my profession."

He says: "Are you going back now? To the park?"

"Yes. She may be waiting."

"I thought she was looking at the lake."

"When she is not looking at the lake, then she is in the park."

The catechist reaches into the sleeve of his black robe. He produces a manifesto. He reads me the manifesto. "*All intellectual productions of the bourgeoisie are either offensive or defensive weapons against the revolution. All intellectual productions of the bourgeoisie are, objectively, obfuscating objects which are obstacles to the emancipation of the proletariat.*" He replaces the manifesto in his sleeve.

I say: "But there are levels of signification other than the economic involved."

The catechist opens his book. He reads: "*A disappointing experience: the inadequacy of language to express thought. But let the catechist take courage.*" He closes the book.

I think: Courage.

He says: "What do you propose to do?"

I say: "I suggested to her that I might change my profession."

"Have you had an offer?"

"A feeler."

"From whom?"

"General Foods."

"How did she respond?"

"A chill fell upon the conversation."

"But you pointed out—"

"I pointed out that although things were loosening up it would doubtless be a long time before priests were permitted to marry."

The catechist looks at me.

I think: She is waiting in the park, in the children's playground.

He says: "And then?"

I say: "I heard her confession."

"Was it interesting?"

"Nothing new. As you know, I am not permitted to discuss it."

"What were the others doing?"

"Tormenting the mothers."

"You wrote another letter?"

"Yes."

"You don't tire of this activity, writing letters?"

"One does what one can." I think: Or does not do what one can.

He says: "Let us discuss love."

I say: "I know nothing about it. Unless of course you refer to Divine love."

"I had in mind love as it is found in the works of Scheler, who holds that love is an aspect of phenomenological knowledge, and Carroll, who holds that 'tis love, 'tis love, that—"

"I know nothing about it."

The catechist opens his book. He reads: *"How to deal with the educated. Temptation and scandals to be faced by the candidate during his catechumenate."* He closes the book. There is never a day, never a day, on which we do not have this conversation. He says: "When were you ordained?"

I say: "1950."

He says: "These sins, your own, the sins we have been discussing, I'm sure you won't mind if I refer to them as sins although their magnitude, whether they are mortal or venial, I leave it to you to assess, in the secret places of your heart—"

I say: "One sits in the confessional hearing confessions, year after year, Saturday after Saturday, at four in the afternoon, twenty-one years times fifty-two Saturdays, excluding leap year—"

"One thousand and ninety-two Saturdays—"

"Figuring forty-five adulteries to the average Saturday—"

"Forty-nine thousand one hundred and forty adulteries—"

"One wonders: Perhaps there should be a redefinition? And with some adulteries there are explanations. The man is a cabdriver. He works nights. His wife wants to go out and have a good time. She tells him that she doesn't do anything wrong—a few drinks at the neighborhood bar, a little dancing. 'Now, you know, Father, and I know, Father, that where there's drinking and dancing there's bloody well something else too. So I tell her, Father, she'll stay out of that bar or I'll hit her upside the head. Well, Father, she says to me you can hit me upside the head all you want but I'm still going to that bar when I want and you can hit me all day long and it won't stop me. Now, what can I do, Father? I got to be in this cab every night of the week except Mondays and sometimes I work Mondays to make a little extra. So I hit her upside the head a few times but it don't make any difference, she goes anyhow. So I figure, Father, she's getting it outside the home, why not me? I'm always sorry after, Father, but what can I do? If I had a day job it would be different and now she just laughs at me and what can I do, Father?' "

"What do you say?"

"I advise self-control."

The catechist pokes about in his pockets. He pokes in his right-hand pocket for a time and then pokes in his left-hand pocket. He produces at length a tiny Old Testament, a postage-stamp Old Testament. He opens the postage-stamp Old Testament. *"Miserable comforters are ye all."* He closes the postage-stamp Old Testament. "Job 16:2." He replaces the postage-stamp old Testament in his left-hand pocket. He pokes about in his right-hand pocket and produces a button on which the word LOVE is printed. He pins the button on my cassock, above the belt, below the collar. He says: "But you'll go there again."

I say: "At eleven. The children's playground."

He says: "The rain. The trees."

I say: "All that rot."

He says: "The benches damp. The seesaw abandoned."

I say: "All that garbage."

He says: "Sunday the day of rest and worship is hated by all classes of men in every country to which the Word has been carried. Hatred of Sunday in London approaches one hundred percent. Hatred of Sunday in Rio produces suicides. Hatred of Sunday in Madrid is only appeased by the ritual slaughter of large black animals, in rings. Hatred of Sunday in Munich is the stuff of legend. Hatred of Sunday in Sydney is considered by the knowledgeable to be hatred of Sunday at its most exquisite."

I think: She will press against me with her hands in the back pockets of her trousers.

The catechist opens his book. He reads: *"The apathy of the listeners. The judicious catechist copes with the difficulty."* He closes the book.

I think: Analysis terminable and interminable. I think: Then she will leave the park looking backward over her shoulder.

He says: "And the guards, what were they doing?"

I say: "Abusing the mothers."

"You wrote a letter?"

"Another letter."

"Would you say, originally, that you had a vocation? Heard a call?"

"I heard many things. Screams. Suites for unaccompanied cello. I did not hear a call."

"Nevertheless—"

"Nevertheless I went to the clerical-equipment store and purchased a summer cassock and a winter cassock. The summer cassock has short sleeves. I purchased a black hat."

"And the lady's husband?"

"He is a psychologist. He works in the limits of sensation. He is attempting to define precisely the two limiting sensations in the sensory continuum, the upper limit and the lower limit. He is often at the lab. He is measuring vanishing points."

"An irony."

"I suppose."

There is no day on which this conversation is not held and no detail of this conversation which is not replicated on any particular day on which the conversation is held.

The catechist produces from beneath his cloak a banner. He unfurls the banner and holds the unfurled banner above his head with both hands. The banner says, YOU ARE INTERRUPTED IN THE MIDST OF MORE CONGENIAL WORK? BUT THIS IS GOD'S WORK. The catechist refurls the banner. He replaces the banner under his cloak. He says: "But you'll go there again?"

I say: "Yes. At eleven."

He says: "But the rain . . ."

I say: "With her hands in the back pockets of her trousers."

He says: *Deo gratias.*

The Flight of Pigeons
from the Palace

In the abandoned palazzo, weeds and old blankets filled the rooms. The palazzo was in bad shape. We cleaned the abandoned palazzo for ten years. We scoured the stones. The splendid architecture was furbished and painted. The doors and windows were dealt with. Then we were ready for the show.

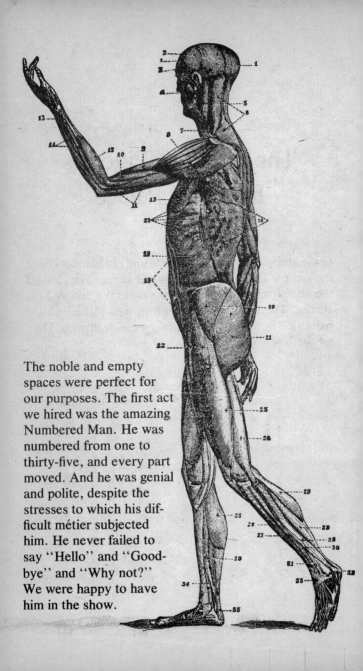

The noble and empty spaces were perfect for our purposes. The first act we hired was the amazing Numbered Man. He was numbered from one to thirty-five, and every part moved. And he was genial and polite, despite the stresses to which his difficult métier subjected him. He never failed to say ''Hello'' and ''Goodbye'' and ''Why not?'' We were happy to have him in the show.

Then, the Sulking Lady was obtained. She showed us her back. That was the way she felt. She had always felt that way, she said. She had felt that way since she was four years old.

We obtained other attractions—a Singing Sword and a Stone Eater. Tickets and programs were prepared. Buckets of water were placed about, in case of fire. Silver strings tethered the loud-roaring strong-stinking animals.

The lineup for opening night included:

A startlingly handsome man
A Grand Cham
A tulip craze
The Prime Rate
Edgar Allan Poe
A colored light

We asked ourselves: How can we improve the show?

We auditioned an explosion.

There were a lot of situations where men were being evil to women—dominating them and eating their food. We put those situations in the show.

In the summer of the show, grave robbers appeared in the show. Famous graves were robbed, before your eyes. Winding-sheets were unwound and things best forgotten were remembered. Sad themes were played by the band, bereft of its mind by the death of its tradition. In the soft evening of the show, a troupe of agoutis performed tax evasion atop tall, swaying yellow poles. Before your eyes.

The trapeze artist with whom I had an understanding . . . The moment when she failed to catch me . . .

Did she really try? I can't recall her ever failing to catch anyone she was really fond of. Her great muscles are too deft for that. Her great muscles at which we gaze through heavy-lidded eyes . . .

We recruited fools for the show. We had spots for a number of fools (and in the big all-fool number that occurs immediately after the second act, some specialties). But fools are hard to find. Usually they don't like to admit it. We settled for gowks, gulls, mooncalfs. A few babies, boobies, sillies, simps. A barmie was engaged, along with certain dum-dums and beefheads. A noodle. When you see them all wandering around, under the colored lights, gibbering and performing miracles, you are surprised.

I put my father in the show, with his cold eyes. His segment was called, My Father Concerned About His Liver.

Performances flew thick and fast.

We performed The Sale of the Public Library.

We performed Space Monkeys Approve Appropriations.

We did Theological Novelties and we did Cereal Music (with its raisins of beauty) and we did not neglect Piles of Discarded Women Rising from the Sea.

There was faint applause. The audience huddled together. The people counted their sins.

Scenes of domestic life were put in the show.

We used The Flight of Pigeons from the Palace.

It is difficult to keep the public interested.

The public demands new wonders piled on new wonders.

Often we don't know where our next marvel is coming from.

The supply of strange ideas is not endless.

The development of new wonders is not like the production of canned goods. Some things appear to be wonders in the beginning, but when you become familiar with them, are not wonderful at all. Sometimes a seventy-five-foot highly paid cacodemon will raise only the tiniest *frisson*. Some of us have even thought of folding the show—closing it down. That thought has been gliding through the hallways and rehearsal rooms of the show.

The new volcano we have just placed under contract seems very promising . . .

The Rise of Capitalism

The first thing I did was make a mistake. I thought I had understood capitalism, but what I had done was assume an attitude—melancholy sadness—toward it. This attitude is not correct. Fortunately your letter came, at that instant. "Dear Rupert, I love you every day. You are the world, which is life. I love you I adore you I am crazy about you. Love, Marta." Reading between the lines, I understood your critique of my attitude toward capitalism. Always mindful that the critic must *"studiare da un punto di vista formalistico e semiologico il rapporto fra lingua di un testo e codificazione di un—"* But here a big thumb smudges the text—the thumb of capitalism, which we are all under. Darkness falls. My neighbor continues to commit suicide, once a fortnight. I have his suicides geared into my schedule because my role is to save him; once I was late and he spent two days unconscious on the floor. But now that I have understood that I have not understood capitalism, perhaps a less equivocal position toward it can be "hammered out." My daughter demands more Mr. Bubble for her bath. The shrimp boats lower their nets. A book called *Humorists of the 18th Century* is published.

•

Capitalism places every man in competition with his fellows for a share of the available wealth. A few people accumulate big piles, but most do not. The sense of community falls victim to this struggle. Increased abundance and prosperity are tied to growing "productivity." A hierarchy of functionaries interposes itself between the people and the leadership. The good of the private corporation is seen as prior to the public good. The world market system tightens control in the capitalist countries and terrorizes the Third World. All things are manipulated to these ends. The King of Jordan sits at his ham radio, inviting strangers to the palace. I visit my assistant mistress. "Well, Azalea," I say, sitting in the best chair, "what has happened to you since my last visit?" Azalea tells me what has happened to her. She has covered a sofa, and written a novel. Jack has behaved badly. Roger has lost his job (replaced by an electric eye). Gigi's children are in the hospital being detoxified, all three. Azalea herself is dying of love. I stroke her buttocks, which are perfection, if you can have perfection, under the capitalistic system. "It is better to marry than to burn," St. Paul says, but St. Paul is largely discredited now, for the toughness of his views does not accord with the experience of advanced industrial societies. I smoke a cigar, to disoblige the cat.

•

Meanwhile Marta is getting angry. "Rupert," she says, "you are no better than a damn dawg! A plain dawg has more sensibility than you, when it comes to a woman's heart!" I try to explain that it is not my fault but capitalism's. She will have none of it. "I stand behind the capitalistic system," Marta says. "It has given us everything we have—the streets, the parks, the great avenues and boulevards, the promenades and malls—and other things, too, that I can't think of right now." But what has the market been doing? I scan the list of the fifteen Most Loved Stocks:

Occident Pet	983,100	20⅝	+	3¾
Natomas	912,300	58⅜	+	18½

What chagrin! Why wasn't I into Natomas, as into a fine garment, that will win you social credit when you wear it to the ball? I am not rich again this morning! I put my head between Azalea's breasts, to hide my shame.

•

Honoré de Balzac went to the movies. He was watching his favorite flick, *The Rise of Capitalism*, with Simone Simon and Raymond Radiguet. When he had finished viewing the film, he went out and bought a printing plant, for fifty thousand francs. "Henceforth," he said, "I will publish myself, in handsome expensive de-luxe editions, cheap editions, and foreign editions, duodecimo, sextodecimo, octodecimo. I will also publish atlases, stamp albums, collected sermons, volumes of sex education, remarks, memoirs, diaries, railroad timetables, daily newspapers, telephone books, racing forms, manifestos, libretti, abecedaries, works on acupuncture, and cookbooks." And then Honoré went out and got drunk, and visited his girl friend's house, and, roaring and stomping on the stairs, frightened her husband to death. And the husband was buried, and everyone stood silently around the grave, thinking of where they had been and where they were going, and the last handfuls of wet earth were cast upon the grave, and Honoré was sorry.

•

The Achievements of Capitalism:
  (a) The curtain wall
  (b) Artificial rain
  (c) Rockefeller Center
  (d) Casals
  (e) Mystification

•

"Capitalism sure is sunny!" cried the unemployed Laredo toolmaker, as I was out walking, in the streets of Laredo. "None of that noxious Central European mis-erabilism for us!" And indeed, everything I see about me seems to support his position. Laredo is doing very well now, thanks to application of the brilliant princi-ples of the "new capitalism." Its Gross Laredo Product is up, and its internal contradictions are down. Catfish-farming, a new initiative in the agri-business sector, has worked wonders. The dram-house and the card-house are each nineteen stories high. "No mat-ter," Azalea says. "You are still a damn dawg, even if you have 'unveiled existence.' " At the Laredo Coun-try Club, men and women are discussing the cathedrals of France, where all of them have just been. Some liked Tours, some Lyon, some Clermont. "A pious fear of God makes itself felt in this spot." Capitalism arose and took off its pajamas. Another day, another dollar. Each man is valued at what he will bring in the marketplace. Meaning has been drained from work and assigned instead to remuneration. Unemployment obliterates the world of the unemployed individual. Cultural underdevelopment of the worker, as a technique of domination, is found everywhere under late capitalism. Authentic self-determination by individuals is thwarted. The false consciousness created and catered to by mass culture perpetuates ignorance and powerlessness. Strands of raven hair floating on the surface of the Ganges . . . Why can't they clean up the Ganges? If the wealthy capitalists who operate the Ganges wig factories could be forced to install sieves, at the mouths of their plants . . . And now the sacred Ganges is choked with hair, and the river no longer knows where to put its flow, and the moonlight on the Ganges is swallowed by the hair, and the water darkens. By Vishnu! This is an intolerable situation! Shouldn't something be done about it?

•

Friends for dinner! The *crudités* are prepared, green and fresh . . . The good paper napkins are laid out . . . Everyone is talking about capitalism (although some people are talking about the psychology of aging, and some about the human use of human beings, and some about the politics of experience). "How can you say that?" Azalea shouts, and Marta shouts, "What about the air?" As a flower moves toward the florist, women move toward men who are not good for them. Self-actualization is not to be achieved in terms of another person, but you don't know that, when you begin. The negation of the negation is based on a correct reading of the wrong books. The imminent heat-death of the universe is not a bad thing, because it is a long way off. Chaos is a position, but a weak one, related to that "unfocusedness" about which I have forgotten to speak. And now the saints come marching in, saint upon saint, to deliver their message! Here are St. Albert (who taught Thomas Aquinas), and St. Almachius (martyred trying to put an end to gladiatorial contests), and St. Amadour (the hermit), and St. Andrew of Crete (whose "Great Kanon" runs to two hundred and fifty strophes), and St. Anthony of the Caves, and St. Athanasius the Athonite, and St. Aubry of the Pillar, and many others. "Listen!" the saints say. "He who desires true rest and happiness must raise his hope from things that perish and pass away and place it in the Word of God, so that, cleaving to that which abides forever, he may also together with it abide forever." Alas! It is the same old message. "Rupert," Marta says, "the embourgeoisment of all classes of men has reached a disgusting nadir in your case. A damn hawg has more sense than you. At least a damn hawg doesn't go in for 'the bullet wrapped in sugar,' as the Chinese say." She is right.

•

Smoke, rain, abulia. What can the concerned citizen do to fight the rise of capitalism, in his own community? Study of the tides of conflict and power in a system in which there is structural inequality as an important task. A knowledge of European intellectual history since 1789 provides a useful background. Information theory offers interesting new possibilities. Passion is helpful, especially those types of passion which are non-licit. Doubt is a necessary precondition to meaningful action. Fear is the great mover, in the end.

The Temptation of
St. Anthony

Yes, the saint was underrated quite a bit, then, mostly by people who didn't like things that were ineffable. I think that's quite understandable—that kind of thing can be extremely irritating, to some people. After all, everything is hard enough without having to deal with something that is not tangible and clear. The higher orders of abstraction are just a nuisance, to some people, although to others, of course, they are quite interesting. I would say that on the whole, people who didn't like this kind of idea, or who refused to think about it, were in the majority. And some were actually angry at the idea of sainthood—not at the saint himself, whom everyone liked, more or less, except for a few, but about the idea he represented, especially since it was not in a book or somewhere, but actually present, in the community. Of course some people went around saying that he "thought he was better than everybody else," and you had to take these people aside and tell them that they had misperceived the problem, that it wasn't a matter of simple conceit, with which we are all familiar, but rather something pure and mystical, from the realm of the extraordinary, as it were; unearthly. But a lot of people don't like things that are unearthly, the things of this earth are good enough for them, and they don't mind telling you so. "If he'd just go out and get a job, like everybody else, then he could be saintly all day long, if he wanted to"—that was a common theme. There is a sort of hatred going around for people who have lifted their sights above the common run. Probably it has always been this way.

For this reason, in any case, people were always trying to see the inside of the saint's apartment, to find out if strange practices were being practiced there, or if you could discern, from the arrangement of the furniture and so on, if any had been, lately. They would ring the bell and pretend to be in the wrong apartment, these people, but St. Anthony would let them come in anyhow, even though he knew very well what they were thinking. They would stand around, perhaps a husband-and-wife team, and stare at the rug, which was ordinary beige wall-to-wall carpet from Kaufman's, and then at the coffee table and so on, they would sort of slide into the kitchen to see what he had been eating, if anything. They were always surprised to see that he ate more or less normal foods, perhaps a little heavy on the fried foods. I guess they expected roots and grasses. And of course there was a big unhealthy interest in the bedroom, the door to which was usually kept closed. People seemed to think he should, in pursuit of whatever higher goals he had in mind, sleep on the floor; when they discovered there was an ordinary bed in there, with a brown bedspread, they were slightly shocked. By now St. Anthony had made a cup of coffee for them, and told them to sit down and take the weight off their feet, and asked them about their work and if they had any children and so forth: they went away thinking, He's just like anybody else. That was, I think, the way he wanted to present himself, at that time.

———————

Later, after it was all over, he moved back out to the desert.

———————

I didn't have any particular opinion as to what was the right thing to think about him. Sometimes you have to take the long way round to get to a sound consensus, and of course you have to keep the ordinary motors of life running in the meantime. So, in that long year that saw the emergence of his will as one of its major landmarks, in our city, I did whatever I could to help things along, to direct the stream of life experience at him in ways he could handle. I wasn't a disciple, that would be putting it far too strongly; I was sort of like a friend. And there were things I could do. For example, this town is pretty goodsized, more than a hundred thousand, and in any such town—maybe more so than in the really small ones, where everyone is scratching to survive—you run into people with nothing much to do who don't mind causing a little trouble, if that would be diverting, for someone who is unusual in any way. So the example that Elaine and I set, in more or less just treating him like any one of our other friends, probably helped to normalize things, and very likely protected him, in a sense, from some of the unwelcome attentions he might otherwise have received. As men in society seem to feel that the problem is to get all opinions squared away with all other opinions, or at least in recognizable congruence with the main opinion, as if the world were a jury room that no one could leave until everybody agreed (and keeping in mind the ever-present threat of a mistrial), so the men, and the women too, of the city (which I won't name to spare possible embarrassment to those of the participants who still live here) tried to think about St. Anthony, and by extension saintliness, in the approved ways of their time and condition.

The first thing to do, then, was to prove that he was a fake. Strange as it may sound in retrospect, that was the original general opinion, because who could believe that the reverse was the case? Because it wasn't easy, in the midst of all the other things you had to think about, to imagine the marvelous. I don't mean that he went around doing tricks or anything like that. It was just a certain—ineffable is the only word I can think of, and I have never understood exactly what it means, but you get a kind of feeling from it, and that's what you got, too, from the saint, on good days. (He had his ups and downs.) Anyhow, it was pretty savage, in the beginning, the way the local people went around trying to get something on him. I don't mean to impugn the honesty of these doubters; doubt is real enough in most circumstances. Especially so, perhaps, in cases where what is at issue is some principle of action: if you believe something, then you logically have to act accordingly. If you decided that St. Anthony actually was a saint, then you would have to act a certain way toward him, pay attention to him, be reverent and attentive, pay homage, perhaps change your life a bit. So doubt is maybe a reaction to a strong claim on your attention,

one that has implications for your life-style, for change.
And you absolutely, in many cases, *don't want* to do
this. A number of great plays have demonstrated this
dilemma, on the stage.

———————

St. Anthony's major temptation, in terms of his living
here, was perhaps this: ordinary life.

———————

Not that he proclaimed himself a saint in so many
words. But his actions, as the proverb says, spoke
louder. There was the ineffableness I've already mentioned, and there were certain things that he did. He
was mugged, for example. That doesn't happen too
often here, but it happened to him. It was at night,
somebody jumped on him from behind, grabbed him
around the neck and began going through his pockets.
The man only got a few dollars, and then he threw St.
Anthony down on the sidewalk (he put one leg in front
of the saint's legs and shoved him) and then began to run
away. St. Anthony called after him, held up his hand,
and said, "Don't you want the watch?" It was a good
watch, a Bulova. The man was thunderstruck. He
actually came back and took the watch off St. Anthony's wrist. He didn't know what to think. He
hesitated for a minute and then asked St. Anthony if he
had bus fare home. The saint said it didn't matter, it
wasn't far, he could walk. Then the mugger ran away
again. I know somebody who saw it (and of course did
nothing to help, as is common in such cases). Opinion
was divided as to whether St. Anthony was saintly, or
simpleminded. I myself thought it was kind of dumb of

him. But St. Anthony explained to me that somebody had given him the watch in the first place, and he only wore it so as not to hurt that person's feelings. He never looked at it, he said. He didn't care what time it was.

Parenthetically. In the desert, where he is now, it's very cold at night. He won't light a fire. People leave things for him, outside the hut. We took out some blankets but I don't know if he uses them. People bring him the strangest things, electric coffee pots (even though there's no electricity out there), comic books, even bottles of whiskey. St. Anthony gives everything away as fast as he can. I have seen him, however, looking curiously at a transistor radio. He told me that in his youth, in Memphis (that's not Memphis, Tennessee, but the Memphis in Egypt, the ruined city) he was very fond of music. Elaine and I talked about giving him a flute or a clarinet. We thought that might be all right, because performing music, for the greater honor and glory of God, is an old tradition, some of our best music came about that way. The whole body of sacred music. We asked him about it. He said no, it was very kind of us but it would be a distraction from contemplation and so forth. But sometimes, when we drive out to see him, maybe with some other people, we all sing hymns. He appears to enjoy that. That appears to be acceptable.

A funny thing was that, toward the end, the only thing he'd say, the only word was . . . "Or." I couldn't understand what he was thinking of. That was when he was still living in town.

_____

The famous temptations, that so much has been written about, didn't occur all that often while he was living amongst us, in our city. Once or twice. I wasn't ever actually present during a temptation but I heard about it. Mrs. Eaton, who lived upstairs from him, had actually drilled a hole in the floor, so that she could watch him! I thought that was fairly despicable, and I told her so. Well, she said, there wasn't much excitement in her life. She's fifty-eight and both her boys are in the Navy. Also some of the wood shavings and whatnot must have dropped on the saint's floor when she drilled the hole. She bought a brace-and-bit specially at the hardware store, she told me. "I'm shameless," she said. God knows that's true. But the saint must have known she was up there with her fifty-eight-year-old eye glued to the hole. Anyhow, she claims to have seen a temptation. I asked her what form it took. Well, it wasn't very interesting, she said. Something about advertising. There was this man in a business suit talking to the saint. He said he'd "throw the account your way" if the saint would something something. The only other thing she heard was a mention of "annual billings in the range of five to six mil." The saint said no, very politely, and the man left, with cordialities on both sides. I asked her what she'd been expecting and she looked at me with a gleam in her eye and said: "Guess." I suppose she meant women. I myself was curious, I admit it, about the fabulous naked beauties he is supposed to have been tempted with, and all of that. It's hard not to let your imagination become salacious, in this context. It's funny that we never seem to get enough of sexual things, even though Elaine and I have been very happily married for nine years and have a very good relationship, in bed and out of it. There never seems to be enough sex in a person's life, unless you're exhausted and worn out, I suppose—that is a curiosity, that God made us that way, that I have never understood. Not that I don't enjoy it, in the abstract.

———————

After he had returned to the desert, we dropped by one day to see if he was home. The door of his hut was covered with an old piece of sheepskin. A lot of ants and vermin were crawling over the surface of the sheepskin. When you go through the door of the hut you have to move very fast. It's one of the most unpleasant things about going to see St. Anthony. We knocked on the sheepskin, which is stiff as a board. Nobody answered. We could hear some scuffling around inside the hut. Whispering. It seemed to me that there was more than one voice. We knocked on the sheepskin again; again nobody answered. We got back into the Pontiac and drove back to town.

———————

Of course he's more mature now. Taking things a little easier, probably.

———————

I don't care if he put his hand on her leg or did not put his hand on her leg.

———————

Everyone felt we had done something wrong, really wrong, but by that time it was too late to make up for it.

———————

Somebody got the bright idea of trying out Camilla on him. There are some crude people in this town. Camilla is well known. She's very aristocratic, in a way, if "aristocratic" means that you don't give a damn what kind of damn foolishness, or even evil, you lend yourself to. Her folks had too much money, that was part of it, and she was too beautiful—she was beautiful, it's the only word—that was the other part. Some of her friends put her up to it. She went over to his place wearing those very short pants they wore for a while, and all of that. She has beautiful breasts. She's very intelligent, went to the Sorbonne and studied some kind of philosophy called "structure" with somebody named Levy who is supposed to be very famous. When she came back there was nobody she could talk about it to. She smokes a lot of dope, it's well known. But in a way, she is not uncompassionate. She was interested in the saint for his own personality, as well as his being an anomaly, in our local context. The long and short of it is that she claimed he tried to make advances to her, put his hand on her leg and all that. I don't know if she was lying or not. She could have been. She could have been telling the truth. It's hard to say. Anyhow a great hue was raised about it and her father said he was going to press charges, although in the event, he did not. She stopped talking about it, the next day. Probably something happened but I don't necessarily think it was what she said it was. She became a VISTA volunteer later and went to work in the inner city of Detroit.

Anyhow, a lot of people talked about it. Well, what if

he *had* put his hand on her leg, some people said—what was so wrong about that? They were both unmarried adult human beings, after all. Sexuality is as important as saintliness, and maybe as beautiful, in the sight of God, or else why was it part of the Divine plan? You always have these conflicts of ideas between people who think one thing and people who think another. I don't give a damn if he put his hand on her leg or did not put his hand on her leg. (I would prefer, of course, that he had not.) I thought it was kind of a cheap incident and not really worth talking about, especially in the larger context of the ineffable. There really was something to that. In the world of mundanity in which he found himself, he *shone*. It was unmistakable, even to children.

———

Of course they were going to run him out of town, by subtle pressures, after a while. There is a lot of anti-clericalism around, still. We visit him, in the desert, anyhow, once or twice a month. We missed our visits last month because we were in Florida.

———

He told me that, in his old age, he regarded the temptations as "entertainment."

Daumier

We Have All
Misunderstood
Billy the Kid

I was speaking to Amelia.

"Not self-slaughter in the crude sense. Rather the construction of surrogates. Think of it as a transplant."

"Daumier," she said, "you are not making me happy."

"The false selves in their clatter and boister and youthful brio will slay and bother and push out and put to all types of trouble the original, authentic self, which is a dirty great villain, as can be testified and sworn to by anyone who has ever been awake."

"The self also dances," she said, "sometimes."

"Yes," I said, "I have noticed that, but one pays dear for the occasional schottische. Now, here is the point about the self: It is insatiable. It is always, always hankering. It is what you might call rapacious to a fault. The great flaming mouth to the thing is never in this world going to be stuffed full. I need only adduce the names of Alexander, Richelieu, Messalina, and Billy the Kid.''

"You have misunderstood Billy the Kid," she murmured.

"Whereas the surrogate, the construct, is in principle satiable. We design for satiability."

"Have you taken action?" she asked. "Or is all this just the usual?"

"I have one out now," I said, "a Daumier, on the plains and pampas of consciousness, and he is doing very well, I can tell you that. He has an important post in a large organization. I get regular reports."

"What type of fellow is he?"

"A good true fellow," I said, "and knows his limits. He doesn't overstep. Desire has been reduced in him to a minimum. Just enough left to make him go. Loved and respected by all."

"Tosh," she said. "Tosh and bosh."

"You will want one," I said, "when you see what they are like."

"We have all misunderstood Billy the Kid," she said in parting.

A LONG SENTENCE
IN WHICH THE
MIRACLE OF SURROGATION
IS PERFORMED
BEFORE YOUR EYES

Now in his mind's eye which was open for business at all times even during the hours of sleep and dream and which was the blue of bedcovers and which twinkled and which was traced with blood a trifle at all times and which was covered at all times with a monocle of good quality, the same being attached by long thin black streamy ribands to his mind's neck, now in this useful eye Daumier saw a situation.

MR. BELLOWS,
MR. HAWKINS,
THE TRAFFIC,
CHILIDOGS

Two men in horse-riding clothes stood upon a plain, their attitudes indicating close acquaintance or colleagueship. The plain presented in its foreground a heavy yellow oblong salt lick rendered sculptural by the attentions over a period of time of sheep or other salt-loving animals. Two horses in the situation's upper left-hand corner watched the men with nervous horse-gaze.

Mr. Bellows spoke to his horse.

"Stand still, horse."

Mr. Hawkins sat down atop the salt lick and filled a short brass pipe Oriental in character.

"Are they quiet now?"

"Quiet as the grave," Mr. Bellows said. "Although I don't know what we'll be doin' for quiet when the grass gives out."

"That'll be a while yet."

"And Daumier?"

"Scoutin' the trail ahead," said Mr. Hawkins.

"He has his problems you must admit."

"Self-created in my opinion."

Mr. Hawkins took a deep draw upon his pipelet.

"The herd," he said.

"And the queen."

"And the necklace."

"And the cardinal."

"It's the old story," Mr. Hawkins stated. "One word from the queen and he's off tearing about the countryside and let business go hang."

"There's such a thing as tending to business, all right," said Mr. Bellows. "Some people never learned it."

"And him the third generation in the Traffic," Mr. Hawkins added. Then, after a moment: "Lovely blue flowers there a while back. I don't suppose you noticed."

"I noticed," said Mr. Bellows. "I picked a bunch."

"Did you, now. Where are they at?"

"I give um to someone," Mr. Bellows said.

"Someone. What someone?"

There was a silence.

"You are acquainted with the Rules, I believe," Mr. Hawkins said.

"Nothing in the Rules about bestowal of bluebonnets, I believe," Mr. Bellows replied.

"Bluebonnets, were they? Now, that's nice. That's very nice."

"Bluebonnets or indeed flowers of any kind are not mentioned in the Rules."

"We are promised to get this here shipment—"

"I have not interfered with the shipment."

"We are promised to get this here herd of *au-pair* girls to the railhead intact in both mind and body," Mr. Hawkins stated. "And I say that bestowal of bluebonnets is interferin' with a girl's mind and there's no two ways about it."

"She was looking very down-in-the-mouth."

142

"Not your affair. Not your affair."

Mr. Bellows moved to change the subject. "Is Daumier likely to be back for chow do you think?"

"What is for chow?"

"Chilidogs."

"He'll be back. Daumier does love his chilidog."

Résumé of the Plot
or Argument

Ignatius Loyola XVIII, with a band of hard-riding fanatical Jesuits under his command, has sworn to capture the herd and release the girls from the toils so-called of the Traffic, in which Daumier, Mr. Hawkins, and Mr. Bellows are prominent executives of long standing. Daumier meanwhile has been distracted from his proper business by a threat to the queen, the matter of the necklace (see Dumas, *The Queen's Necklace*, pp. 76–105).

Description of
Three O'Clock
in the Afternoon

I left Amelia's place and entered the October afternoon. The afternoon was dying giving way to the dark night, yet some amount of sunglow still warmed the cunning-wrought cobbles of the street. Many citizens both male and female were hurrying hither and thither on errands of importance, each *agitato* step compromising slightly the sheen of the gray fine-troweled sidewalk. Immature citizens in several sizes were massed before a large factorylike structure where advanced techniques transformed them into true-thinking right-acting members of the three social classes, lower, middle, and upper middle. Some number of these were engaged in ludic agon with basketballs, the same being hurled against passing vehicles producing an unpredictable rebound. Dispersed amidst the hurly and burly of the children were their tenders, shouting. Inmixed with this broil were ordinary denizens of the quarter—shopmen, *rentiers,* churls, sellers of vicious drugs, stum-drinkers, aunties, girls whose jeans had been improved with appliqué rose blossoms in the cleft of the buttocks, practicers of the priest hustle, and the like. Two officers of the Shore Patrol were hitting an imbecile Sea Scout with long shapely well-modeled nightsticks under the impression that they had jurisdiction. A man was swearing fine-sounding swearwords at a small yellow motorcar of Italian extraction, the same having joined its bumper to another bumper, the two bumpers intertangling like shameless lovers in the act of love. A man in the organic-vegetable hustle stood in the back of a truck praising tomatoes, the same being abulge with tomato-muscle and ablaze with minimum daily requirements. Several members of the madman profession made the air sweet with their imprecating and their moans and the subtle music of the tearing of their hair.

THOUGHT

Amelia is skeptical, I thought.

LIST OF RESEARCH
MATERIALS CONSULTED

My plan for self-transplants was not formulated without the benefit of some amount of research. I turned over the literature, which is immense, the following volumes sticking in the mind as having been particularly valuable: *The Self: An Introduction* by Meyers, *Self-Abuse* by Samuels, *The Armed Self* by Crawlie, Burt's *The Concept of Self, Self-Congratulation* by McFee, Fingarette's *Self-Deception, Self-Defense for Women and Young Girls* by Birch, Winterman's *Self-Doubt, The Effaced Self* by Lilly, *Self-Hatred in Vermin* by Skinner, LeBett's *Selfishness,* Gordon's *Self-Love, The Many-Colored Self* by Winsor and Newton, Paramananda's *Self-Mastery, The Misplaced Self* by Richards, *Nastiness* by Bertini, *The Self Prepares* by Teller, Flaxman's *The Self as Pretext,* Hickel's *Self-Propelled Vehicles,* Sørensen's *Self-Slaughter, Self and Society in Ming Thought* by DeBary, *The Sordid Self* by Clute, and *Techniques of Self-Validation* by Wright. These works underscored what I already knew, that the self is a dirty great villain, an interrupter of sleep, a deviler of awakeness, an intersubjective atrocity, a mouth, a maw. Transplantation of neutral or partially inert materials into the cavity was in my view the one correct solution.

NEUTRAL OR PARTIALLY
INERT MATERIALS
CROSS A RIVER

A girl appeared holding a canteen.

"Is there any wine *s'il vous plaît?*"

"More demands," said Mr. Hawkins. "They accumulate."

"Some people do not know they are a member of a herd," said Mr. Bellows.

The girl turned to Daumier.

"Is it your intention to place all of us in this dirty water?" she asked, pointing to the river. "Together with our clothes and personal belongings as well?"

"There is a ford," said Daumier. "The water is only knee-high."

"And on the other bank, shooters? Oh, that's very fine. *Très intelligent.*"

"What's your name, Miss?"

"Celeste," said the girl. "Possibly there are vipers in the water? Poisonmouths?"

"Possibly," said Daumier. "But they won't hurt you. If you see one, just go around him."

"Myself, I will stay here, thank you. The other girls, they stay here too, I think."

"Celeste, you wouldn't be telling them about poisonmouths in the water, would you?"

"It is not necessary. They can look for their own selves." She paused. "Possibly you have a very intelligent plan for avoiding the shooters?"

She is not pretty, Daumier thought. But a good figure.

"My papa is a lawyer," she said. "An *avocat.*"

"So?"

"There was no word in the agreement about marching through great floods filled with vipers and catfishes."

"The problem is not the water but the Jesuits on the other side," said Daumier.

"The noble Loyola. Our resuscitator."

"You want to spend the next year in a convent? Wearing a long dress down to your feet and reading *The Lives of the Saints* and not a chilidog to your name?"

"He will take us to the convent?"

"Yes."

"What a thing. I did not know."

"Daumier," said Mr. Hawkins. "What is your *très intelligent* plan?"

"What if we send some of the girls in to bathe?"

"What for?"

"And while the enemy is struck blind by the dazzling beauty of our girls bathing, we cross the rest of them down yonder at the other ford."

"Ah, you mean bathing, uh—"

"Right."

"Could you get them to do it?"

"I don't know." He turned to Celeste. "What about it?"

"There is nothing in the agreement about making Crazy Horse shows in the water. But on the other hand, the cloister . . ."

"Yes," said Daumier.

Soon seven girls wearing towels were approaching the water.

"You and Mr. Bellows cross the herd down there. I'll watch out for these," Daumier said to Mr. Hawkins.

"Oh, you will," said Mr. Hawkins. "That's nice. That's very nice indeed. That is what I call nice, that is."

"Mr. Hawkins," said Daumier.

Then Daumier looked at Celeste and saw that the legs on her were as long and slim as his hope of Heaven and the thighs on her were as strong and sweet-shaped as ampersands and the buttocks on her were as pretty as two pictures and the waist on her was as neat and incurved as the waist of a fiddle and the shoulders on her were as tempting as sex crimes and the hair on her was as long and black as Lent and the movement of the whole was honey, and he sank into a swoon.

When he awoke, he found Mr. Hawkins lifting him by

his belt and lowering him to the ground again, repeatedly.

"A swoon most likely," said Mr. Hawkins. "He was always given to swoonin'."

The girls were gathered about him, fully dressed and combing their damp hair.

"He looks extremely charming when he is swooned," said Celeste. "I don't like the eagle gaze so much."

"And his father and grandfather before him," said Mr. Hawkins, "they were given to swoonin'. The grandfather particularly. Physical beauty it was that sent the grandfather to the deck. There are those who have seen him fall at the mere flash of a kneecap."

"Is the herd across?" asked Daumier.

"Every last one of um," said Mr. Hawkins. "Mr. Bellows is probably handing out the TV dinners right now."

"We made a good exhibition, I think," said Celeste. "Did you see?"

"A little," said Daumier. "Let's push across and join the others."

They crossed the river and climbed a ridge and went through some amount of brush and past a broke-down abandoned farmhouse with no roof and through a pea patch that nobody had tended for so many years that the peas in their pods were as big as Adam's apples. On the other side of the pea patch they found Mr. Bellows tied to a tree by means of a great many heavy ropes around his legs, stomach, and neck and his mouth stuffed full of pages torn from a breviary. The herd was nowhere to be seen.

* * *

Two Whiskeys
with a Friend

"The trouble with you," said Gibbon, "is that you are a failure."

"I am engaged upon a psychological thimblerig which may have sound commercial applications," I said. "Vistas are opening."

"Faugh," he said.

"Faugh?"

"The trouble with you is that you are an idiot," Gibbon said. "You lack a sense of personal worthlessness. A sense of personal worthlessness is the motor that drives the overachiever to his splendid overachievements that we all honor and revere."

"I have it!" I said. "A deep and abiding sense of personal worthlessness. One of the best."

"It was your parents I expect," said Gibbon. "They were possibly too kind. The family of orientation is charged above all with developing the sense of personal worthlessness. Some are sloppy about it. Some let this responsibility slide and the result is a child with no strong sense of personal worthlessness, thus no drive to prove that the view he holds of himself is not correct, the same being provable only by conspicuous and distinguished achievement above and beyond the call of reasonableness."

I thought: His tosh is better than my tosh.

"I myself," said Gibbon, "am slightly underdone in the personal worthlessness line. It was Papa's fault. He used no irony. The communications mix offered by the parent to the child is as you know twelve percent do this, eighty-two percent don't do that, and six percent huggles and endearments. That is standard. Now, to avoid boring himself or herself to death during this monition the parent enlivens the discourse with wit, usually irony of the cheaper sort. The irony ambigufies the message, but more importantly establishes in the child the sense of personal lack-of-worth. Because the child understands that one who is talked to in this way is not much of a something. Ten years of it goes a long way. Fifteen is better. That is where Pap fell down. He eschewed irony. Did you bring any money?''

"Sufficient.''

"Then I'll have another. What class of nonsense is this that you are up to with the surrogate?''

"I have made up a someone who is taking the place of myself. I think about him rather than about me.''

"The trouble with you is that you are simpleminded. No wonder you were sacked from your job in the think tank.''

"I was thinking but I was thinking about the wrong things.''

"Does it work? This transplant business?''

"I have not had a thought about myself in seven days.''

"Personally,'' said Gibbon, "I am of the opinion that the answer is Krishna Socialism.''

MR. BELLOWS
IS SPRUNG;
ARRIVAL OF
A FIGURE;
POPCORN AVAILABLE
IN THE LOWER LOBBY

"Our herd is rustled,'' said Mr. Hawkins.

Mr. Bellows was having pages of the Word removed from his mouth.

"Fifteen hundred head," said Daumier. "My mother will never forgive me."

"How many men did he have with him?" asked Mr. Hawkins.

"Well I only *saw* about four. Coulda been more. They jumped me just as we come outa the tree line. Two of 'em come at me from the left and two of 'em come at me from the right, and they damn near pulled me apart between 'em. And himself sittin' there on his great black horse with the five black hats on him and laughin' and gigglin' to beat all bloody hell. Then they yanked me off my horse and throwed me to the ground terrible hard and two of 'em sat on me while himself made a speech to the herd."

"What type of speech would that be?"

"It begun, 'Dearly beloved.' The gist of it was that Holy Mother the Church had arranged to rescue all the girls from the evil and vicious and low and reprehensible toils of the Traffic—meaning us—and the hardships and humiliations and degradations of *au-pair* life through the God-smiled-upon intervention of these hard-riding pure-of-heart Jesuits."

"How did the herd take it?"

"Then he said confessions would be between two and four in the afternoon, and that evening services would be at eight sharp. Then there was a great lot of groanin'. That was from the herd. Then the girls commenced to ask the padres about the hamburger ration and the grass ration and which way was the john and all that, and the boys in black got a little bit flustered. They realized they had fifteen hundred head of ravenous *au-pair* girls on their hands."

"He seems a good thinker," said Celeste. "To understand your maneuver beforehand, and to defeat it with his own very much superior maneuver—"

At that moment a figure of some interest approached

the group. The figure was wearing on the upper of his two lips a pair of black fine-curled mustachios and on the top of his head a hat with a feather or plume of a certain swash and on his shoulders a cape of dark-blue material of a certain swagger and on his trunk a handsome leather doublet with pot-metal clasps and on the bottom of him a pair of big blooming breeches of a peach velvet known to interior decorators for its appositeness in the upholstering of loveseats and around his waist a sling holding a long resplendent rapier and on his two hands great gauntlets of pink pigskin and on his fine-chiseled features an expression of high-class arrogance. The figure was in addition mounted upon the top of a tall-standing well-curried fast-trotting sheep.

"What is it?" asked Mr. Bellows.

"Beats me," said Mr. Hawkins. "I think it is an actor."

"I know what it is," said Daumier. "It is a musketeer."

FURTHER BOILING
OF THE PLOT
IN SUMMARY FORM

The musketeer carries a letter from the queen which informs Daumier that Jeanne de Valois, a bad person attached to the court, has obtained the necklace, which is worth 1,600,000 francs, by persuading the Cardinal de Rohan, an admirer of the queen, to sign a personal note for the amount, he thinking he is making a present to the queen, she thinking that the necklace has been returned to the jewelers, Jeanne de Valois having popped the diamonds into an unknown hiding place. The king is very likely going to find out about the whole affair and become very angry, in several directions. Daumier is begged to come to the capital and straighten things out. He does so.

HISTORY OF THE SOCIETY OF JESUS

Driven from England, 1579
  Driven from France, 1594
  Driven from Venice, 1606
  Driven from Spain, 1767
  Driven from Naples, 1768
  Suppressed entirely by Clement XIV, 1773
  Revived, 1814

SOMETHING IS HAPPENING

I then noticed that I had become rather fond—fond to a fault—of a person in the life of my surrogate. It was of course the girl Celeste. My surrogate obviously found her attractive and no less did I; this was a worry. I began to wonder how I could get her out of his life and into my own.

AMELIA OBJECTS

"What about me?"

QUOTATIONS FROM LA FONTAINE

"I must have the new, though there be none left in the world."

The Parry

"You are insatiable," she said.

"I am in principle fifty percent sated," I said. "Had I two surrogates I would be one hundred percent sated. Two are necessary so that no individual surrogate gets the big head. My identification with that Daumier who is even now cleaning up all sorts of imbroglios in the queen's service is wonderful but there must be another. I see him as a quiet, thoughtful chap who leads a contemplative-type life. Maybe in the second person."

The New Surrogate
Given a Trial Run

This is not the worst time for doing what you are doing, and you are therefore pleased with yourself—not wildly, but a little. There are several pitfalls you have avoided. Other people have fallen into them. Standing at the rim of the pit, looking down at the sharpened stakes, you congratulate yourself on your good luck (because you know good sense cannot be credited) and move on. The conditions governing your life have been codified and set down in a little book, but no one has ever given you a copy, and when you have sought it in libraries, you are told that someone else has it on extended loan. Still, you are free to seek love, to the best of your ability, or to wash your clothes in the machines that stand with their round doors temptingly open, or to buy something in one of the many shops in this area—a puppy perhaps. Pausing before a show window full of puppies, brown and black and mixtures, you notice that they are very appealing. If only you could have one that would stay a puppy, and not grow into a full-sized dog. Your attachments are measured. Not that you are indifferent by nature—you want nothing so much as a deep-going, fundamental involvement—but this does not seem to happen. Your attachments are measured; each seems to last exactly two years. Why is that? On the last lap of a particular liaison, you feel that it is *time to go,* as if you were a guest at a dinner party and the host's offer of another brandy had a peculiar falseness to it. Full of good will, you attempt to pretend that you do not feel this way, you attempt to keep the level of cheerfulness and hope approximately where it has always been, to keep alive a sense of "future." But no one is fooled. Optimistic plans are made, but within each plan is another plan, allowing for the possible absence of one of the planners. You eye the bed, the record-player, the pictures, already making lists of who will take what. What does this say about you—that you move from person to person, a tourist of the emotions? Is this the meaning of failure? Perhaps it is too soon to decide. It has occurred to you that you, Daumier, may yet do something great. A real solid durable something, perhaps in the field of popular music, or light entertainment in general. These fields are not to be despised, although you are aware that many people look down on them. But perhaps a better-conceived attack might contain a shade less study. It is easy to be satisfied if you get out of things what inheres in them, but you must look closely, take nothing for granted, let nothing become routine. You must fight against the cocoon of habituation which covers everything, if you let it. There are always openings, if you can find them. There is always something to do.

* * *

A Sampling of
Critical Opinion

"He can maunder."

"Can't he maunder!"

"I have not heard maundering of this quality since—"

"He is a maundering fool."

Celeste Motors
from One Sphere
to Another Sphere

"She has run away," said Mr. Hawkins.

"Clean as a whistle," said Mr. Bellows.

"Herd-consciousness is a hard thing to learn," said Mr. Hawkins. "Some never learn it."

"Yes," said Mr. Bellows, "there's the difficulty, the iddyological. You can get quite properly banjaxed there, with the iddyological."

Food

I was preparing a meal for Celeste—a meal of a certain elegance, as when arrivals or other rites of passage are to be celebrated.

First off there were Saltines of the very best quality and of a special crispness, squareness, and flatness, obtained at great personal sacrifice by making representations to the National Biscuit Company through its authorized nuncios in my vicinity. Upon these was spread with a hand lavish and not stinting Todd's Liver

Pâté, the same having been robbed from geese and other famous animals and properly adulterated with cereals and other well-chosen extenders and the whole delicately spiced with calcium propionate to retard spoilage. Next there were rare cheese products from Wisconsin wrapped in gold foil in exquisite tints with interesting printings thereon, including some very artful representations of cows, the same being clearly in the best of health and good humor. Next there were dips of all kinds including clam, bacon with horseradish, onion soup with sour cream, and the like, which only my long acquaintance with some very high-up members of the Borden company allowed to grace my table. Next there were Fritos curved and golden to the number of 224 (approx.), or the full contents of the bursting 53¢ bag. Next there were Frozen Assorted Hors d'Oeuvres of a richness beyond description, these wrested away from an establishment catering only to the nobility, the higher clergy, and certain selected commoners generally agreed to be comers in their particular areas of commonality, calcium propionate added to retard spoilage. In addition there were Mixed Nuts assembled at great expense by the Planters concern from divers strange climes and hanging gardens, each nut delicately dusted with a salt that has no peer. Furthermore there were cough drops of the manufacture of the firm of Smith Fils, brown and savory and served in a bowl once the property of Brann the Iconoclast. Next there were young tender green olives into which ripe red pimentos had been cunningly thrust by underpaid Portuguese, real and true handwork every step of the way. In addition there were pearl onions meticulously separated from their nonstandard fellows by a machine that had caused the Board of Directors of the S. & W. concern endless sleepless nights and had passed its field trials just in time to contribute to the repast I am describing. Additionally there were gherkins whose just fame needs no further words from me. Following these appeared certain cream cheeses of Philadelphia origin wrapped in costly silver foil, the like of which a pasha could not have afforded in the dear dead days. Following were Mock Ortolans Manqués made of the very best soybean aggregate, the like of which could not be found on the most sophisticated tables of Paris, London, and Rome. The whole washed down with generous amounts of Tab, a fiery liquor brewed under license by the Coca-Cola Company which will not divulge the age-old secret recipe no matter how one begs and pleads with them but yearly allows a small quantity to circulate to certain connoisseurs and bibbers whose credentials meet the very rigid requirements of the Cellar-master. All of this stupendous feed being a mere scherzo before the announcement of the main theme, chilidogs.

"What is all this?" asked sweet Celeste, waving her hands in the air. "Where is the food?"

"You do not recognize a meal spiritually prepared," I said, hurt in the self-love.

"We will be very happy together," she said. "I cook."

Conclusion

I folded Mr. Hawkins and Mr. Bellows and wrapped them in tissue paper and put them carefully away in a drawer along with the king, the queen, and the cardinal. I was temporarily happy and content but knew that there would be a time when I would not be happy and content; at that time I could unwrap them and continue their pilgrimages. The two surrogates, the third-person

Daumier and the second-person Daumier, were wrapped
in tissue paper and placed in the drawer; the second-
person Daumier especially will bear watching and
someday when my soul is again sickly and full of
sores I will take him out of the drawer and watch him.
Now Celeste is making a *daube* and I will go into the
kitchen and watch Celeste making the *daube*. She is
placing strips of optional pork in the bottom of a pot.
Amelia also places strips of optional pork in the bottom
of a pot, when she makes a *daube,* but somehow— The
self cannot be escaped, but it can be, with ingenuity and
hard work, distracted. There are always openings, if
you can find them, there is always something to do.